THE DAY
EAZY-E
DIED

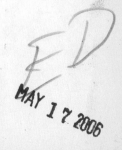

Other titles by the author
available from Alyson Books

B-Boy Blues
2nd Time Around
If Only for One Nite
Back 2 Back

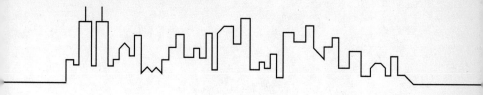

THE DAY
EAZY-E
DIED

JAMES EARL HARDY

alyson books
los angeles | new york

© 2001 BY JAMES EARL HARDY. ALL RIGHTS RESERVED

MANUFACTURED IN THE UNITED STATES OF AMERICA.

THIS TRADE PAPERBACK IS PUBLISHED BY ALYSON PUBLICATIONS,
P.O. BOX 4371, LOS ANGELES, CALIFORNIA 90078-4371.
DISTRIBUTION IN THE UNITED KINGDOM BY TURNAROUND PUBLISHER SERVICES LTD.,
UNIT 3, OLYMPIA TRADING ESTATE, COBURG ROAD, WOOD GREEN,
LONDON N22 6TZ ENGLAND.

FIRST EDITION PUBLISHED IN HARDCOVER BY ALYSON BOOKS: AUGUST 2001
FIRST PAPERBACK EDITION: AUGUST 2002

02 03 04 05 06 **a** 10 9 8 7 6 5 4 3 2 1

ISBN 1-55583-760-3

LIBRARY OF CONGRESS CATALOGING-IN-PUBLICATION DATA
    HARDY, JAMES EARL.
        THE DAY EAZY-E DIED / JAMES EARLY HARDY.—1ST ED.
        ISBN 1-55583-760-3 (PAPERBACK); ISBN 1-55583-509-0 (HARDCOVER)
        1. AIDS (DISEASE)—DIAGNOSIS—FICTION. 2. MALE MODELS—FICTION.
        3. GAY MEN—FICTION. I. TITLE.
    PS3558.A62375 D39 2001
    813'.54—DC21   2001035769

COVER DESIGN BY MATT SAMS.
COVER PHOTOGRAPHY BY DINO DINCO.

JEH's Thank-U's...

The Director...
of my work, of my world–**God**

The Crew...
Mi Familia y Amigos, who carry me and carry on with me. I Love U All!
Bam Bam...a jood, understanding (God)son
Lonnie Elle Walker...a jood Brutha and friend
Abdur-Rahim Briggs...a "Pooquie" of a Brutha
James E. Houston, Jr., my *soul-full* mate
Ricc Rollins & Lorenzo Robertson, 4 their dedication, commitment, inspiration, and brotherhood

Joshua Alston, my pimp papi

Tori Fixx, who is doing what many in hip hop aren't—*keepin' it real*

Dwayne Jenkins of Brothers United/Nashville, 4 his sound advice

TQ, my Supa Sweet, Chocolate Chunk, Honey Dip, Luva Boyee-U really know how 2 Take Care of Bizness!

My e-mail pals and gals the world over, 4 your unwavering support and patience!

The Contributors 2 the Soundtrack...

Aaliyah, Yolanda Adams, Erykah Badu, Eric Benet, Mary J. Blige, Da Brat, Toni Braxton, Deborah Cox, D'Angelo, Missy "Misdemeanor" Elliot, Faith Evans, Macy Gray, Lauryn Hill, Whitney Houston, janet, Joe, Chaka Khan, Lil' Kim, Kenny Lattimore, Rahsaan Patterson, Kelly Price, Busta Rhymes, Sandra St. Victor, Jill Scott (ya better know who she is!), Sisqo, Angie Stone, Carl Thomas, TLC, and, of course, Aretha & Randy

&, Once Again,

The Stars...

Pooquie, Little Bit, & Li'l Brotha Man, 4 allowing me the privilege of producing yet another chapter in their lives.

For all the souls we've lost...
and all the souls we must save

1995

Ya make a little green and tha entire world wants a piece of it.

Ever since I got my first phat check from All-American, them credit card applications been comin in like cray-zee. Gold this, Platinum that, Classic this, Optima that. Since I could remember all tha mail I ever received—notices from the Board of Elections, a Xmas card ev'ry year from Mel of Mel's Messenger's, my last check from Simply Dope fuh some artwork I did, and a letter I once got from a cousin I ain't never met—their courtin my bizness made me feel kinda special. Tha Kid likes attention, and they was doin a jood job of holdin it.

But I ain't never had a credit card and wasn't too keen about gettin one now. I done heard too many horror stories about folks goin deep in debt buyin a whole lota shit on credit. My Moms always be maxin her cards out 'round Xmas and be complainin in January and February about them bills. But at least she don't be fallin behind in them payments. Too many folks default, and as soon as ya know it, they got collection agencies callin them day and night, at home and at work, harrassin 'em. I remember seein some report about one woman who said her son was told by a bill collector that if she didn't pay, he was gonna be placed in foster care.

Of course, too many folks just be tryin ta live beyond they means, miscalculatin what they can afford ta pay— and when. Payin sumthin off on time might seem like a jood idea, but once them finance charges start addin up, you be payin much mo' in tha end than if you had just shelled it all out up front.

Which is why I always subscribed ta tha cash 'n' carry plan: If I ain't got tha cash, I ain't carryin it out tha store.

But now that I was in a whole new tax bracket (ha, I don't even think I was *in* one befo'), them cards would come in handy. I wasn't about ta walk around wit' thousands of dollars in my pockets (wit' folks in da 'hood seein my face all over, that'd be stoopid). And, since I was a travelin man now, I might have an emergency on da road.

So, I got tha usual suspects: a Master Card, a Visa, and a Am Ex. But I treat 'em all like cash cards. Wit' Am Ex, you got no choice; you buy sumthin and you know you gonna hafta pay it off in full when that next bill comes. But I use tha other two tha same way, so I don't hafta worry about payin no finance charge. Becuz of my great payment history, they all decided ta increase my available credit (sumthin Little Bit says almost never happens after just six months as a customer), which really is another way of tryin ta get me ta charge mo'—increasin tha chance that I'll decide one month ta only pay that minimum so they can really make some money off my ass. But it's bad enuff they want you ta pay fuh tha so-called privilege of usin *their* card. As far as I'm concerned, that application or annual fee is tha *only* int'rest they gonna be earnin off me.

Of course, once tha word got out that I had these three, ev'rybody else came at me wit' a vengeance. A few even called me up tryin ta persuade me ta sign up (like, how tha fuck they get my number?). But what I need wit' two or three diff'rent MCs or Visas?

I just knew I'd get a reprieve movin inta my new spot—a spacious three bedroom duplex wit' two bathrooms in a co-op called Harlem Towers that's not far from where I grew up. I useta deliver packages here at least twice a week when I was still makin my rounds. I always said I wanted ta live there someday—and now I am. Cuz of my connections (Troy Fauntleroy, my agent, lives in one of tha buildings) and my profile (both tha women *and* tha men in tha office knew who I was and was all too happy ta please me), management is lettin me rent tha place fuh a year. I know they hopin I'll buy it, but I ain't—if I'm gonna spend 65 g's on a piece of property, it's gonna be a house. I got my eye on a brownstone. But I gotta figure out how and when I'm gonna ask Little Bit ta move in wit' me 'n' Li'l Brotha Man (yeah, I know, there are some thangz I gotta do and say first ta other folks befo' sumthin like *that* happens…)

Anyway, I got back from a overnite trip ta D.C., filmin my fifth commercial fuh All-American, and *what* was waitin fuh me? Six new offers in my mailbox (as well as a Hallmark from Little Bit, wishin me jood luck in my first apartment) and three messages on my voice mail wit' them same old folks repeatin them same old lines: "You've Been Pre-Approved!" "Don't Pass Up This Chance of a Lifetime!" "Build That Credit History with a Company You Can Trust!" "No Fees, No Hassles, No Problems!" Day-um, I ain't even been here three days yet and these muthafuckas done tracked my ass down. And, how tha fuck they get *this* number? Tha bitch is s'pose ta be unlisted. Ya think they'd get tha message that I ain't int'rested.

I can see, tho', how folks get caught up in it. I mean, they do make it all sound so jood and simple. I'd be lyin if I said I ain't been tempted ta splurge now and then, or pay that minimum instead of that full amount (especially if it's over a thou'). But I can always hear Little Bit's voice: "Be practical, Pooquie." And I ain't bein practical if I spend $2,000 on a fly Brooks Brothers suit or $5,000 on a 24-karat, diamond-studded ring when I know them funds could go ta better use.

Besides, I got an apartment ta furnish.

I only got a TV, VCR, stereo, a dresser, a nightstand, and a bed, which is where I was sittin, rippin up all these "once-in-a-lifetime offers" (as a few of them claimed). I then started flippin thru a Seaman's circular ta see about livin room sets my Moms said I should check out, when tha phone rang. I let my answerin machine come on, cuz it might be one of them credit card peops. Li'l Brotha Man recorded tha message:

"Hello. You've reached 555-0102. Please leave a message after the beep, and your call will be returned as soon as possible. Thank you."

BEEP...

"Yo, Raheim, it's me, Angel, I—"

I picked up tha receiver. "Yeah, I'm here. Whazzup?"

"Yo, you heard?"

"Heard what?"

"About Eazy-E."

"Eazy? What about him?"

"Uh...he...he got AIDS."

"Hunh?" I knew he didn't just say what he said.

"He got AIDS."

I let out a nervous laugh. "Man, what tha fuck you talkin 'bout? How can Eazy have AIDS?"

"That's what they just said."

"They? They who?"

"Folks on TV. I was just flippin channels and saw it."

"You...you sure you heard right?"

"Yeah. Shit, man, ain't no way you gonna hear sumthin like that wrong."

Silence.

"Yo, Raheim, you there?"

"Uh, yeah, yeah, I'm here. *Day-um*. He got AIDS?"

"Yup."

"He in tha hospital?"

"I don't know."

"Is he in Compton?"

"I don't know."

"How they say he doin?"

"I don't know."

"Nigga, what tha fuck *do* you know?"

"Yo, man, chill. I caught it when it was goin off."

"Oh. Uh, sorry brotha."

"S'a'ight."

"Day-um. I, I can't believe it."

"Yo, I can't believe it, either. I mean, I tripped over my feet when I heard it. I just knew I was hearin thangz."

"Yo, that shit is fucked up."

"You ain't lyin."

"Uh, thanks, man. Thanks fuh tellin me."

"You welcome. Yo, if I hear anything else, I'll letcha know."

"A'ight. Thanks."

"You got it, brotha."

I just sat there fuh a few minutes. Yeah, I was in shock. Ya never think you'll hear sumthin like that. Well, you never think you'll hear that sumthin *like* that happens ta somebody you...well, I can't say *know* cuz I don't know him. And I can't say *like* cuz it's not like I like him.

Admire him? I guess that's tha word. I admire what he managed ta become given what he was up against, what stood in his way. And...*day-um*. He ain't old. He young. He too fuckin young ta be dyin. He too fuckin young ta be dyin of *that*.

I snatched tha remote and tried ta find sumthin on any channel about it but couldn't. But I knew this wasn't gonna be tha only time I heard about it.

M

e 'n' Little
Bit spent tha day makin love wit'out makin love.

We woke up at 8 but stayed in bed 'til noon, wrapped
up in each other's arms, talkin and laughin. We took a
30-minute shower. We fed each other grapes, strawber-
ries, cherries, and orange and banana slices fuh lunch.
We watched *Bloodsport* (yeah, it was my millionth time
seein it and Little Bit's first—and, ta my su'prise, he
liked it) and *The Birds* (which tripped me tha fuck out;
I ain't never gonna look at a pigeon tha same way again).
I enjoyed watchin him cook one of my fav'rite meals—
smothered chicken, peas and rice, collard greens, home-

made biscuits, and a sweet potato pie—and he enjoyed watchin me eat it. Then he watched while I washed tha dishes. We played Scrabble (he won) and *Jeopardy!* (yeah, I'm still tha Champ). And we capped it all off wit' a one-hour hot oil bath.

We was in bed—he between my legs readin a magazine, me skimmin thru *The Wall Street Journal* (now that I was an official member of that six-figure club, I had ta keep up wit' them Joneses)—when...

"Pooquie?"

"Yeah?"

"Listen to this..."

"I hope it ain't nuthin about O.J."

"No, it's not."

"Jood, cuz I could care less about that mutha-fucka."

"I know."

"He all people wanna talk about and I'm *sick* of it."

"I know."

"He gettin just what he deserve, fuckin around wit' that white girl. Now he see what happens when you blinded by tha white."

"Are you quite through? It's not about him, OK?"

"Ah, a'ight. Go 'head."

"It's this news item. The Center for Disease Control says one out of every 90 Black and Hispanic men between the ages of 18 and 30 in urban cities like New York, Washington D.C., Philadelphia, Detroit, and Atlanta are HIV-positive."

"Hunh?"

"That's what it says."

"Baby, you know you can't believe ev'rythang you read, especially when it's in sumthin white."

"Well, this is *Emerge*."

"Ah."

He sighed. "That's frightening. One in 90."

I shrugged. "It ain't true."

"Why not?"

"Cuz it's too fuckin high. It's gotta be a guesstimate."

"A guesstimate?"

"Yeah. You know they always gotta play wit' them digits when it comes ta us. There ain't that many of us that's gonna just give up info like that. So they must be projectin. Besides, given who is rattlin off them figures, I wouldn't put no stock in 'em."

"What do you mean?"

"Baby, we talkin about the Center for Disease *Control*. They ain't inta gettin rid of diseases, but controllin 'em, maintainin 'em. Otherwise, they be outa jobs."

"Hmm…well, considering all the people I've known who have died from it, I can believe it."

"You know a lota people who died from it?"

"Yeah. Well, I should really say I know *of* a lot of people who have died from it. Only one person who was really close to me did."

"You mean yo' uncle?"

"Yes."

"Nobody else?"

"No. Everybody else was either an acquaintance—

somebody you just see when you're out—or a friend of a friend. And that friend has usually been Gene. He's watched most of the people he met when he first came to New York in the late '70s die."

"Day-um. Gene, he a ancient mutha-fucka," I snickered.

He poked me in my side. "Given that he is still around, I'm sure he would consider that a compliment."

"Comin from me? I don't think so."

"He would, believe me. He knows he's blessed. He won't admit it, though."

"Whatcha mean?"

"Well, he doesn't believe in God…at least that's what he says."

"You think he do?"

"Yeah, I do. I mean, how could he not? It's like that old saying, 'There but for the grace of God go I.' He was just as wild and carefree as his friends who have passed on and he's still here. I know there's no other explanation for it. And I think deep down inside he knows it, too."

"Uh, how come you think he don't fess up?"

"Because Gene thinks he has all the answers and only he is in control of his life. Many of us are like that. We think we are invincible. I bet that's how many of those brothers think who end up being one of those statistics. Maybe the situation with Eazy-E can wake some of them up."

I sighed. "Yeah."

"I know you're a fan of his."

I nodded. "Ya know it. I mean, tha brotha was on it.

That science he dropped about life in da 'hood was da bomb. And he just waved his dick all up in white folks' faces, ain't give a shit. But he was really a smart-azz biznessman, too, crankin his soundz out on his own label."

He leaned back, nudgin me. "You don't have to talk about him in the past tense, Pooquie. He's not dead."

I ain't realize I was. "Oh…ah, yeah."

"I'm sure it won't surprise you, but I've never been into his music."

"Nah, it don't surprise me."

"That life…I just didn't grow up around that. And you know how I feel about the *n* word, no matter *how* it's spelled."

I chuckled. "Don't fuhget about tha *b* word and tha *h* word."

"Thanks for reminding me. But I can definitely see why folks were attracted to him."

I leaned up, nudgin him. "They still are, Baby. Remember, he ain't dead."

"Oh, yeah. Sorry. I may not like what he's done musically or agree with some of the things he's said publicly, but I have to give him his props: He's a very courageous man."

"In what way, Baby?"

"Well, he didn't have to disclose his status. Most celebrities who have AIDS or are HIV-positive don't, especially if they're Black. It's not until after they're gone that we find out. Hmph, sometimes we don't even find out then. You have to figure it out by reading between the lines."

"How?"

"For one thing, the obituary. They'll say the cause of death was pneumonia or heart failure. It may be what they died from, but then you see that they were so young. It's usually a dead giveaway...no pun intended. You'd think after Magic...it's four years later and the stigma is still there. I remember those stories I did, interviewing brothers about what they thought and whether his announcement would change the way they see AIDS and people who have it. Naturally, they all said yes. But as those stats imply, knowin about Magic hasn't really raised awareness that much. So, hopefully, with Eazy coming out..."

I nearly leapt outa bed. "*Comin out?* Baby, what tha *fuck* you talkin 'bout?"

He pushed me back. "Pooquie, will you calm down? I'm not saying he's gay. I think he made it clear that he isn't, saying he contracted the virus through unprotected heterosexual sex."

"It don't sound like you believe him."

"Well, I don't really care if he is gay, bi, or tri. I just don't think it was necessary for him to emphasize he got it that way. It doesn't matter how he got it."

"C'mon, Little Bit, you know that's a lie. It does too matter ta folks how you get it."

"Well, it shouldn't, and the last thing he should be worrying about when he's fighting for his life is what people think. Holding on to that heterosexual machismo image isn't gonna make him better."

"Yo, whether he was kickin it wit' another brotha or

not, he know what time it is. He don't wanna lose his place, his standin. That's just tha way it is."

"That might be the way it is, but it's not the way it has to be, Pooquie. Anyway, when I said he was coming out, I was referring to his saying he has AIDS. Too many of these homies and homettes think it can't happen to them. So if his revelation makes one person use a condom the next time they have sex, then his plea won't be in vain."

"Ah...I see whatcha sayin. But you ain't hafta put it like *that.*"

He shook his head. "Pooquie, you are so silly."

"And, can we change tha topic? All this talk about AIDS and Eazy...it's just depressin." And it was.

"Sorry. I brought it up because all of it makes you think."

"About what?"

"Eazy is only 31. He more than likely became infected sometime in his early to mid 20s. And we're in that age range. It could easily be one of us."

"But it ain't us, Baby."

"I know, I know. But...there but for the grace of God, you know?"

"Yeah, I know."

Iplanned ta spend much of my time off doin absolutely nuthin. It's when you get all caught up that you remember how simple thangz useta be. Even them moments I useta have wit' Little Bit—not doin a thang except bein wit' him—done become even mo' special cuz of my hectic schedule.

But I also wanted ta do thangz I hadn't done in some time. So I headed on over ta tha YMCA ta shoot some hoops. Tha last time I was there was prob'ly in March '93 when Brotha Man was still alive. We would go there when it was too damn chilly ta be playin ball at tha courts on West 4th and 6th Ave.

I ain't wanna go by myself, so I called up Angel. But I soon regretted that: I barely beat him in our first two games (21-19 and 21-20) and he trounced me in tha third (21-12). Defeated and disgusted, I called a time-out and plopped down on a bench.

He dribbled over ta me. "Man, I know sumthin must be up wit' you."

"Hunh?"

"Yo, this tha first time I ever beat you. Whazzup?"

"Ain't nuthin up, a'ight?"

He sat down. "Sumthin gotta be up, anytime you miss not one, not two, but *three* of yo' jamfabulous Jordan jump shots."

"Man…it ain't nuthin, a'ight? I don't wanna talk about it."

"Yo, man. It's me, Angel."

"Mutha-fucka, I know who you are, and that's *exactly* why I ain't tellin yo' ass."

"Yo, man, I ain't gonna break no code of silence. You can tell me. I gotcha back. I ain't gonna tell nobody."

"Uh-huh, I heard *that* shit befo'."

"Yo, I been keepin my mouth shut about a whole lota shit. You can trust me."

I considered it. I gave in. "You can't tell *no*-fuckin-body."

"Like, who I'm gonna tell?"

"Uh-huh…well…it's about me 'n' Little Bit."

"What about y'all?"

"Well…this thing wit' Eazy…I can't get it off my mind. It makes ya think…like, if you really know who you wit'…if you really know yo'self."

"Brotha, you ain't got nuthin ta worry about."

"Whatcha mean?"

"You 'n' Little Bit…just like Brotha Man said, you so fuckin lucky ta have him. Y'all been kickin it fuh almost two years 'n' shit. And he *gotta* be sumthin else ta put up wit' yo' ass."

I frowned. "Funny, mutha-fucka, real funny."

He smiled. "You hear me laughin?"

"I…I just…I'm worried about losin him."

"Man, tha only way that shit is gonna happen is…" He glared at me. "Uh-oh. What tha fuck you do?"

"It ain't what I did, it's what I didn't do. I told Little Bit…I told him I had a AIDS test, and I didn't."

"So? It ain't like you got it. You ain't sick, are you?"

"No, I ain't, but that don't mean shit. People walkin 'round ev'ry day wit' it, man. You can't tell. Ever since you told me about Eazy…my mind just been driftin back ta all them times I ain't use a condom."

"But this was way befo' you met him, right?"

"Yeah."

He shrugged. "Then you ain't got nuthin ta worry about."

"I do, too, dummy. That shit can lie 'n' wait fuh yo' ass fuh like 10 years. Just cuz it ain't show up yet don't mean it won't."

"Man, I'm tellin ya, you ain't got nuthin ta worry about."

"Nigga, will you stop sayin that shit? I do, too."

"Man, you been bucklin up wit' him ev'ry time, right?"

My eyebrows raised. "Bucklin up?"

"Yeah. I heard that on *Ricki Lake*."

I chuckled. "Yeah. I been bucklin up wit' him ev'ry time. But that don't mean nuthin. Ain't nuthin a 100% proof."

He nodded. "True. But you ain't been kickin it wit' nobody else, right?"

Silence.

"Right?" he repeated.

"Uh…" I stammered.

"Man, you been gettin buzy wit' somebody else?" He looked like he was gonna jump outa his skin.

"Nah, nah, we ain't been gettin buzy…you know…we just…we just messed around."

His eyebrows raised. "And how messy did it get?"

"Man, we ain't wet no pipes, a'ight? It was just one of those thangz, ya know? He cranked my tool, I cranked his. He scratched me, I scratched him."

"He licked you, you licked him."

"Sumthin like that."

"Who is it?"

"Now, I *ain't* tellin you that, and I don't care if you swore on a Bible or the Koran."

"Why not, man?"

"Cuz, tellin even one person is like breakin his confidence, and I ain't doin that shit ta him."

"A'ight, I hear ya. A nigga wit' a rep ta protect."

"Yeah."

"Cool. But y'all ain't do da do. So, what's tha prob?"

"Tha prob is that I still lied ta Little Bit. I mean, what if…what if I got it and it turns out I gave it ta him?"

"A'ight, a'ight. Say you do got a plus sign and he got one, too, and you *did* give it ta him. How he gonna prove that? You just never know."

"He gonna know and I'm gonna know cuz he had a test just befo' we met. So, if he turn up wit' a plus sign, he gonna know exactly who ta blame."

"Not necessarily. Like you said, you can have it fuh years and not know. Man, I think you sweatin fuh no reason. But if you wanna be sure, you should get a test done."

I sighed. "Yeah. I guess so."

He shrugged. "Ain't no big deal."

"'Ain't no big deal?' Findin out if you gonna *die* ain't no big deal?"

"Man, we *all* gonna die sometime. But it ain't about findin out if you gonna *die*; it's about findin out if you gonna *live*. I know. I had one."

I looked at him, su'prised. "You had a test?"

"Yup."

"When?"

"A year ago. Alicia was takin Anjelica fuh a check-up and felt that, fuh Anjelica's sake, we both find out if we got a clean bill of health. She was gettin tested and she said she wanted me ta, too. But I knew she wanted us ta do it cuz she know I been fuckin other people."

"Yeah, and other people been fuckin you," I chuckled.

"Yeah. And you would know that, right, mutha-fucka?" he snapped back.

Yeah, I do. Gotta admit, he got a sweet azz and know how ta give it up. Day-um, it slipped my mind that we kicked it once. At least he somebody I boned that I can remember, whose name I *know*. Ain't many. "So, this was s'pose ta tell her what she couldn't ask you herself?" I asked, wantin ta get away from there.

"Yup."

"Y'all still wanna get married?"

"No, *she* still wanna get married."

I laughed. "Yeah. Ev'ry time her 'n' Sunshine hook up, that's all she talk about."

"I ain't wanna get no test done. I was like, 'Yo, whatcha tryin ta say about me?' But I ain't do nuthin that would make me think I got a plus sign. I mean, I ain't been givin or givin up nuthin wit'out no glove."

"You mean, you ain't never done it wit'out one?"

He shook his head. "Nope."

I waved him off. "Man, you *gots*ta be lyin."

"No, I ain't."

"You had ta be dippin wit'out it, nigga. How else Alicia have yo' baby?"

"Man, da jimmy broke on us. I knew I shouldn'ta let Alicia put it on. It was her first time and she ain't know what tha fuck she was doin."

"Hmm…I know about breakin-'em-in…me 'n' Sunshine in that club, too. So, you took tha test?"

"Yeah."

"And?"

"And what?"

"You know what. Did you get a plus or a minus sign?"

"Man, that's kinda personal. I mean, even if you swore

not ta tell nobody on a Bible or—"

I elbowed him in tha arm. "Nigga, if you don't tell me, I'll drop yo' ass."

He grinned. "Hmm…I might like that."

I bet he would. "Funny. Just tell me."

"It was a minus."

I puffed out a big sigh. "Ah."

"Yeah. I breathed a *big*-mutha-fuckin sigh of relief over that one, too."

"I thought you wasn't worried about it?"

"I wasn't worried. But when you gotta wait them two weeks ta get them results…man, I'm tellin ya…I knew what they meant by bein on pins 'n' needles. It ain't until you hear it fuh yo'self, you can breathe."

"That shit sounds like torture."

"It was. It is."

"Man, you ain't exactly sellin this AIDS test on me."

"It ain't pretty. It's some serious shit. But I tell you one thang: If you do it, at least yo' mind is gonna be clear. I'm glad I did it."

"You glad?"

"Yeah. It's just like they say: it's better ta know than not know. If Eazy had known he was on tha plus side, he might not be in tha position he in right now."

I nodded in agreement.

"And, I woulda felt bad not doin it. I mean, I wanna make sure I'm around fuh my Anjelica. I wanna see her go ta college."

"Nigga, you gotta potty-train her ass first!"

"Man, you know what I mean."

"Yeah. Yeah, I do."

"And, you just wouldn't be doin it fuh you. You got L'il Brotha Man ta think about, too." He got up. "Ha, you get that plus sign and maybe, *maybe* yo' game'll come back."

"Say what? Nigga, you talkin a whole lota shit fuh somebody who won one game outa tha hundreds I done whipped yo' ass playin."

"Yo, looks like ya winnin streak done ended, my brotha. It's time fuh me ta catch up."

I pointed at him. "Mutha-fucka, you couldn't catch a cold in a snowstorm!"

He dribbled. "Uh, you sweatin, man, you sweatin, and you know what they say: Never let 'em see ya sweat. Ya better save that fuh tha court."

I jumped up. "A'ight, a'ight, put ya gab where ya think yo' gravy is, mutha-fucka. Let's see if you got tha biscuits ta serve wit' that shit. Game 21, and ta show ya how much faith I got, I'll spot yo' ass 10 points."

"Man, I don't need no charity." He bounced tha ball ta me.

I threw it back at him. "Nigga, what tha fuck you think I been doin playin wit' *yo'* ass all this time?"

ou *gots* ta be
jokin?"

Me 'n' my agent, Troy, was havin lunch at the Carlyle.
If there's one jood thang that came outa Little Bit goin
ta his 10th anniversary high school reunion, it was his
runnin inta Troy again. I was just about ta bust up wit'
All-American and needed some representation when he
offered his services. Ta be honest, I ain't think he could
do tha job; after all, he ain't have no experience handlin
a model (all his clients are on Broadway) and that hair-
do he got (a cross between a Mohawk and a fade) ain't
exactly businesslike. I can imagine tha looks on folks'

faces when he shows up fuh a meetin or lunch date (ha, like right now). But if anybody knew that havin a look is tha best way ta get any castin director's eye, whether you tryin out fuh a role in a play or a spot in a commercial, it's him.

And he's figured out how to work my look (ya know us bald, blue-black bruthaz are "in" now) so jood that ain't a week gone by since we hooked up that I ain't been in somebody's studio or on somebody's lot. He's had me walkin, struttin, boppin, runnin, stylin, profilin, smilin, laughin, grinnin, chinnin, spinnin, jumpin, jackin, dribblin, swingin, and swayin my ass off nonstop fuh eight months. Word, I ain't worked so hard so much in all my life (which is why I needed some time off). And, given that models are s'pose ta make that all-important pit stop in Europe, work them runways fuh a few years, get them tear sheets, and *then* come back ta tha USA ta make it Big, I'm one lucky mutha-fucka.

Thanks ta Troy, I'm about ta really blow up. When he heard Fox ("the Negro Network," as he calls it) was lookin fuh somebody ta cohost a music video show, he sent them a tape of me fillin in fuh a VJ on MTV fuh a week. I met tha producers and they liked me. But Troy convinced them ta drop tha other host (yeah, he was white) and build tha show around me. It's s'pose ta premiere in October, Fridays at midnite. Tha Kid'll be checkin in wit' tha crew as they cut new jamz, hangin out wit' folks at their fav'rite spots in New York, and countin down tha top tunes of tha week like Casey Kasem.

And knowin tha right folk and bein tha new (and cheap) kid on da block got me my first movie role, playin one of three high school b-ballers tryin ta make it outa da 'hood and inta the NBA. Now, if *Rebound* sounds a lot like *Hoop Dreams*, that ain't no coincidence. You know how these Follywood folks are: They see a jood thang and they copy it. Troy went ta college wit' one of tha producers and requested an audition. Ya know ev'ry New Jack in Follywood, from Allen Payne ta Larenz Tate, was vyin fuh them slots. But this was an indie (meanin tha budget was pennies compared ta what most films cost these days), so they wasn't about ta shell out a lota green fuh brothas like them. So I was too happy when I was picked. My part was tha smallest of tha three, so my shoot time was quick—two weeks. It'll be out in July.

It ain't been easy, tho', tryin ta find tha right role ta follow it up wit'. After landin such a crop job fuh my debut (I got a free trip, a phat paycheck, and spent much of my time shootin hoops—what mo' could I ask fuh?), I guess I expected mo' of tha same ta be offered ta me. But so far, all tha scripts I been gettin would have me playin some 40-ounce-guzzlin, baby-makin, carjackin, Tech 9–totin, drug-dealin, brotha-droppin nigga—and I ain't goin on like that, ya know what I'm sayin?

So, you'd think Troy would know better than ta even come at me wit' yet another one of them knucklehead hood rock roles.

But he wasn't about ta be dismissed this time. He sat

back, folded his arms across his chest, and made his pitch. "Alright, alright: the tale's been told a million times before, it ain't gonna win any awards, and on the page it's no more than a half-hour of screen time. But it's a high-profile project with a high-profile star, Michelle Pfeiffer."

"You call *her* a star?"

"Yes, my brother, you're a star when you've got three Oscar nominations under your belt and can clock seven figures plus a percentage of the gross. And, you ain't gonna be comin away from the deal empty-handed: They're willing to pay you almost a quarter mill."

Yeah, that sounded jood...*better* than jood. But... "You know tha money ain't important ta me. I just don't wanna be playin no gangsta."

"You won't be."

"C'mon, Troy. What you call it? Tha brotha is criminal-minded."

"Yes, this kid, all the kids in the film have problems. If they didn't, there wouldn't be a movie."

"You know I wanna get a part in a movie I can take my son ta see, where he can be proud of me. This ain't it."

He gave me one of those "Negro, puh-leeze" looks. "Well, as noble as all that sounds and as much as I love to see Li'l Brotha Man smile, this ain't about you makin him proud, this is about you makin a name for yourself, getting all the exposure you can. Just being in this movie with her will raise your profile. And, do I have to remind you that you ain't Eddie Murphy? You're not going to be offered starring roles. You ain't a movie star—yet."

"I know."

He wasn't buyin it. "Do you? It don't seem like it. Just about everything I come up with you turn your nose up at. You gotta work your way up to that level, baby, and people aren't going to consider you for anything bigger or better than this if they don't know you can handle the little stuff first."

I huffed. "I just don't wanna be insultin tha folks."

"How do you know you would be? You haven't even read the script!"

"Yo, that title says it all: *My Posse Don't Do Homework*!"

"Look, it was a best-selling book—"

"Uh-huh, and *who* made it a best-seller? Not *us*."

"Well, somebody must've thought it'd make a good movie, and somebody must've thought *you* would be jood for it: The director specifically asked for *you*."

"Fuh me?"

"Yes. His casting agent worked on *Rebound* and told him how jood you were. And based on that recommendation and the commercial clips and pics I sent him, he believes you are the one for this role. *You're* his first choice. You don't even have to audition; all you have to do is say yes. They've given you 'til Friday to decide. Not many of us catch their eye and move them to offer us a shot like this, so don't waffle."

"But tha story is still bullshit. That's tha bottom line."

"No, the bottom line is this: People love your face— and your body—and they recognize that you have a screen presence. Now they're trying to figure out if you're *more* than a face and a body. And, they're willing to pay you *three* times the money you got for *Rebound* to find out." He pointed ta tha script. "Read it."

I sighed. I picked it up. "A'ight, a'ight. I'll read it."

"Hmph, I know you will. And if you wanna get *your* money's worth out of *me*, I suggest you put your Black pride aside and do it. You act like you went to Yale Drama School and you've been asked to do the Stepin Fetchit Story. All of us gotta start somewhere. Denzel made films like *Carbon Copy* and Laurence Fishburne did stuff like *Death Wish II* before folks would take them seriously. You will, too."

I shrugged.

He picked up his glass of wine. "This is going to open up other doors. And the film will be released in the fall, right around the time your show will debut. I'm tellin' you, it's gonna be a solid one-two punch, comin off the heels of *Rebound*." He sipped.

"So, when they start filmin?"

"Rehearsals begin April 11…"

There goes my vacation…

"And shooting starts April 14. They wrap things up by the third week in May."

"Day-um. They don't waste no time, hunh?"

"Out there, time is indeed money, honey. So they know it can't be wasted. Hell, they already got some of the artists lined up for the soundtrack."

"Oh, yeah? Who?"

"Immature, Craig Mack—"

"Ho, wit' tha flava in ya ear!"

"Yeah. And one of those Jodeci boys is supposed to be doing something solo. I think it's that child who can't keep his shirt on."

I chuckled. "Uh, you mean K-Ci?"

"I guess. It should be against the law for a man to walk around unclothed if he has a chest like a chicken. Eeek!"

We cracked up.

Well, I read tha script—and ya know I ain't like it. And I knew Little Bit wouldn't, either.

We were sprawled out on his sofa, he layin between my legs as he read it. He didn't laugh when he was s'pose ta. He didn't smile when he was s'pose ta. He didn't get choked up and teary-eyed when he was s'pose ta. That frown on his face never changed.

"So, whatcha think?" I asked after he finished, even tho' I already knew what he was gonna say.

He rolled up tha script. He hesitated. "Honest?"

"Yeah, honest. I wouldn't be askin if I didn't want ya ta be."

He sighed. "Well…it's bullshit. This white woman, out of the goodness and kindness of her heart, decides to be a beacon of light in the lives of these poor unfortunate juvenile delinquents in the ghetto. *Puh-leeze*. It's another great white hope story. I mean, there are so many people of color teaching kids of color every day, be they troubled or not, inspiring them to be all they can be, but their stories are never told."

I smiled. "Like you."

He blushed. "Well, I wasn't thinking of me, but you could include me in that group." He tossed tha script on tha coffee table. "They think this woman is Marva Collins, and she ain't. But now that I've vented…you're gonna do it, right?"

"What makes you think I wanna do it?"

"I didn't say you *wanted* to do it; I said you were *going* to do it. Just like before."

"'Just like before?'" Hmm… "A'ight, Little Bit. Let it out."

"Let what out?"

"You know what. You been bailin on me."

"I have not."

"C'mon, Little Bit, we been over this, now…"

"Pooquie…" He put his palms on my bare chest. "It…it really doesn't matter what I think."

I looked at him like he was buggin. "Now, how you gonna say some shit like that?"

"Don't curse at me."

"I ain't curse at you."

"Sounded like it to me."

"Just say it: You don't want me ta do this just like you ain't want me ta do those other things, right?"

He sighed. "OK, OK. If I were in your shoes, I wouldn't have done the ads for Michelob or Newport, and I wouldn't do this movie. Satisfied now?"

I shook my head. "No, I ain't."

"I told you what you wanted to hear, Pooquie."

"I asked you ta tell me what you felt, not what you think I wanted ta hear."

"Well, it's the same thing."

"No, it ain't, Little Bit. You been lyin ta me all these months."

"Lying to you? About what?"

"You ain't been tellin me tha whole truth."

"You asked me what I thought each time, Pooquie, and I told you what I thought. I never lied to you."

"But you wasn't tellin me ev'rythang. I just got a feelin that…that…" I lowered my head. "That you ain't proud of me."

He grasped my chin and lifted my head. He caressed my face. "Pooquie, *how* could you think that? I've been *very* proud of you and the work you've done. Take those ads for the United Negro College Fund and the Big Brothers of America; they were really important. And that cover photo for *American Heritage* magazine: People need to know that there were and are Black cowboys." He smiled. "And you looked too damn jood in that hat."

I grinned. "It turned you on, didn't it?"

"You know it did."

I started ta rise. "You want me ta go get it?"

He pushed me back down, laughin. "No, not right now. Maybe later." His head found its spot on my chest. I held him. "But I wasn't happy about the others because of the way our community is targeted by cigarette and alcohol companies. I didn't feel right about it and I wasn't quiet about it. I told you how I felt. And I just explained why I don't like this movie project. So I told you what I thought, not what I think you should do. That's not my place."

"But I would tell you not ta do sumthin if I thought you shouldn't."

"Ditto."

"'Ditto?' That ain't true, Baby. You talkin outa tha side of yo' neck."

"No, I'm not, Pooquie. I don't necessarily agree with some of the choices you've made. But my not liking those choices and my believing you'd be making a big mistake if you made those choices are two different things. If I felt what you were going to do would do damage to you, I would tell you so and discourage you from doing it. Doing a cigarette or alcohol ad wouldn't—and as we saw didn't—hurt you. In fact, they helped a lot. So, the jood definitely outweighed the bad.

"We're supposed to help the other see the pros and cons so he can make his own decision—even if that decision may impact us both. Like…when I decided I would march in the African-American Day Parade with the Brotherhood in Harlem last year."

"Oh, yeah. I was one wrecked mutha-fucka over that." And I was, too: He was gonna be carryin a sign and shit, all up in tha front of tha troop, so ya know I flipped out.

"Well, I had a right to do it; I didn't need your permission. But you had a right to know and the right to decide how you would handle it because there was a chance it could affect you."

"Yeah. And you did it anyway."

"Yes, I did, for while we should expect the other to compromise in the relationship, we can't expect the other to compromise *himself*. You wouldn't have been able to talk me out of doing it, but I would never have done it without discussing it with you. It was important for us to talk about it, talk it over, talk it out. Well, *I* talked; *you* yelled."

I nudged him wit' my chest. "I ain't yell!"

"You did. I understood where your frustration and fear came from. But in the end, you had nothing to worry about: Your mother and Crystal didn't see me."

"We don't know that," I grunted.

"Now, you know if they did, they would've said something to you about Junior's godfather marchin with fags." He giggled. "And something jood *did* come out of all that fussin and fightin."

"Yeah? What?"

"You were so angry with me that you wouldn't give me none for three weeks. But when you finally got over it, you gave it up—and that shit was Jood with a c-a-p-i-t-a-l *j*. Hmph, debatin the pros and cons with you always pays." He snuggled in tighter.

I moaned. "A'ight, a'ight…so, whatcha think tha pros are fuh this one?"

"Well, this *is* a great opportunity. You do have a few jood lines, and the role will lead to other things. No matter how much the critics pan the movie—and it *will* be panned—it'll still be a hit. It could easily do 70, 80 million. And all that exposure won't hurt the TV series. But I'm sure Troy told you all of this."

"Yeah, he did."

"And, let us not forget the money. A few more offers like this and you will indeed be a millionaire." He sighed. "The real con for me…is that you won't be here for my birthday."

I had already thought of that and had a solution. "Nuthin says you can't come out that weekend."

I could feel him smile.

He squeezed me. "So…you're gonna do it, right?"

I huffed. "Yeah. But how you know I was?"

"I know you, Pooquie. The caution in your voice when you handed me the script…it was like you were hoping I would like it so you'd feel better about doing it. Are you gonna do it for the reasons I mentioned?"

"Yeah," I sighed.

"Well, don't worry. Your principles won't be compromised just because you do this. It's just one role. We all have to do things we don't like or want to do to get to the next level. You'll get the chance to do high-air kicks with Jean-Claude one of these days. And the character may be a hoodlum, but he's an intelligent one. Ha, at least you ain't drivin Miss Daisy or singin the blues for Mr. Charlie."

I chuckled.

"Jooder things will come along. And speaking of jooder things: I saw the Jergens commercial today."

"You did?

"Yup. I got it on tape. It played during *The Young and the Restless.*"

"How ya know it was me, Baby? I mean, they ain't show my face."

He nipped my nipple. "Pooquie, if anyone knows what your chest looks like all soaped up, it's me."

"So...why are you here?"

Jood question. I ain't know what ta say.

Why tha fuck *am* I here? I sho' didn't wanna come up in tha place: I stood across the street fuh like an hour, missin my 12:30 appointment. Hell, I dialed tha phone and hung up a dozen times befo' I talked ta a counselor. And we had ta go over a list of places in two diff'rent states (New Jersey and Connecticut) befo' she named one in Hartford I felt comf'table goin ta and didn't think I'd see anybody I knew (ain't no way I was goin ta one in New York state). But that still ain't make much diff'rence. I was still scared ta go in. I was still scared I was gonna see somebody I knew walkin by. I was still scared I was gonna see somebody I knew comin in or goin outa tha place. I was still scared of what I might find out.

I was just plain *scared*.

But that wind was whippin and that cold air was nippin, so I finally got wise and went on in. But I ain't take off my shades. Five other folks was wearin 'em, too; guess they ain't want nobody spookin them either. One brotha was starin just a little too hard. When it looked like he was gonna ask me if I was *him*, my number was called.

A nurse brought me ta this room. On ev'ry inch of ev'ry wall, in small and big print, in color and black 'n' white...nuthin but AIDS this and AIDS that. I sat down in one of them tacky chairs you see at a welfare office. On this rickety table was some pamphlets and a bowl of condoms.

A tall, cute, light-skinned brotha walked in, lockin up ta give us some privacy. He smiled, sittin down across from me. He said his name was Lenny; it prob'ly wasn't his real name. He told me not ta be nervous, that I'm doin tha right thing comin in fuh counselin. He said he was gonna ask me about my personal life, but I don't hafta be embarrassed. If I don't wanna answer, I don't hafta.

Then he opened up his notebook, got his pen in a take notes position, and asked me that question. He prepped me fuh this, but I was still caught off-guard. Yeah, it was a simple question, but it sure ain't have no simple answer. So, I said tha only thing I could say…

"I…I don't know."

He looked at me, puzzled. "You don't know?"

"Uh…nah."

"Well, there has to be something that brought you here. Has someone you've slept with tested HIV-positive or died from AIDS?"

"No."

"Has someone close to you, a family member or friend, tested HIV-positive or died from AIDS?"

"No."

"Hmm…" He tapped his pen on tha table. "Then it must be Eazy."

How he know? "Uh…yeah."

"Believe me, you're not the only one."

"Whatcha mean?"

"Well, the number of calls about our services has quadrupled since he revealed he's sick. Usually, we see about a dozen people a day. Now, it's twice that. And just like you, most of the folks in that waiting area are hoping no one will recognize them. My guess is those aren't for seeing." He tapped his own prescription glasses.

I shrugged. I took off my shades.

"I just hope your having cold feet didn't make your feet so cold you got frostbite."

"Huh?"

"I saw you, yesterday and today, standing across the street."

BUSTED.

"You…saw me?"

"Yes, but don't sweat it. At least you finally came in. I've seen many who didn't. I only hope they did go somewhere…so, are you a fan of Eazy's?"

"Uh, yeah."

"Me, too. It's a shame. But if it brings more people in to see us and gets them to change their attitude and behavior, I guess there is some good that can come out of tragedy like this." He leaned in toward me. "So, are you afraid you may be HIV-positive?"

"I…I don't know."

"I know you don't, but the possibility that you might be I'm sure is another reason why you're here."

"I…I know I can't be."

"You do? How do you know?"

"Uh, well…I guess I really don't know."

"OK. When was the last time you had sexual intercourse?"

"Last week." And *day-um*, was that shit *jood*. As Angela Winbush (one of our fav'rite sexin CDs) wailed on tha stereo, Little Bit worked on and wore me tha fuck out. Shit, he had me hittin octaves like her.

"Did you and your partner or partners use condoms?"

"Partners?"

"Yes. Some like to swing both ways. Some like to swing *more* than one person. And some like to swing it with more than one person at the *same* time."

"Day-um. Well, I only been swingin wit' one person goin on two years."

"And did you use a condom with her or him during sexual intercourse last week?"

Her *or* him? Hmm…do he know? "Yeah."

"And have you always used a condom with her or him during sexual intercourse?"

"Yeah."

"Always?"

"Yeah."

"Are you sure?"

"Yeah, man, I'm sure. What, you don't believe me?"

"It's not a question of my not believing you. I just want you to be sure, that's all. It's not how many people you've been having sex with, but *how* you've been having sex with them that really matters."

I nodded. "I'm sure."

"OK. What type of sex have you been having with this individual?"

"Type?"

"Yes. Vaginal, anal, oral."

I wasn't about ta spook myself, so… "Vaginal and oral."

"OK. And you used a condom or some other type of protection during each sexual act?"

"Uh…well…no."

"OK. During which one didn't you use protection?"

"Oral."

"Ah…"

"Uh, you s'pose ta use a condom when you have oral sex?"

"Well, the jury is still out on how unsafe it is. It's not

as risky as sharing a needle with someone or having unprotected anal or vaginal sex, but there's still a risk."

Ah shit.

"I take it by the look on your face that you have been having oral sex without a condom?"

"Uh...yeah."

"Well, I know this is gonna sound stupid, but don't worry. Like I said, no one can really say for sure. The real danger is allowing someone to come in your mouth. If you have an open sore in your mouth, there is a chance you can be infected."

I let out a big sigh.

"Was that a sigh of relief or despair?"

I patted my chest. "Relief."

"It's possible, not probable. There aren't many documented cases of it happening."

"Uh...how 'bout...if tha other person is goin down on you?"

"Can they infect you with HIV?"

"Yeah."

"Not likely. But with other sexually transmitted diseases, yes."

"A'ight."

"Have you *ever* had sexual intercourse with someone without using a condom?"

"Uh...uh..."

"Again, you don't have to be embarrassed or ashamed. Most of us have, including me."

"Uh, yeah."

"And this was before you were in your current relationship?"

"Yeah."

"OK. So, if you are HIV-positive, what are you going to do?"

"Huh?"

"What are you going to do? Will you tell the person you're involved with?"

"Yeah."

"Will you tell that person or those people you've had sexual intercourse with?"

That would be impossible since I don't even know where most of them mutha-fuckas I kicked it wit' are. But I said "Yeah" anyway.

"Will you tell your family and friends?"

"Uh…yeah."

His eyebrows raised. "You didn't sound too sure about that one."

"Uh…it…it just ain't gonna be easy."

"No, it won't, but it will be for the best. Walking around with this kind of secret can take a toll on you. If your mind is free from worry, your body and spirit will be, too, and it's very important for a person who is HIV positive to feel that."

I nodded.

"And what about you?"

"Me?"

"Yes, you. What are you going to do for you if you are positive?"

"Whatcha mean?"

"Well, what kind of changes will you make in your life?"

"Changes?"

"Yes. The best way to not get sick—whether you are HIV-positive or not—is to lead a healthy life. You look like you're in very good shape, but you'll have to work at staying that way. Do you exercise on a regular basis?"

"Sho' do. Ev'ry day."

"Good. Lifting weights, I take it?"

"Yeah."

"And your diet. It's important to drink lots of water and juices and eat well-balanced meals."

I had heard that line all my life; I'm sure we all have. And ya know what that means... "You sayin I gotta become a vegetarian?"

"No, but it wouldn't hurt."

"Man, ain't no way I can stop eatin meat!"

He snickered. "I know how you feel. But now, more than ever, you are what you eat. And you'll have to get the right amount of rest. Are you a workaholic?"

"Nah."

"Good. And you get at least eight hours of sleep each night?"

"Uh...not all tha time."

"It's important to. Are you a party animal?"

"Nah. I useta be."

"Good. And you'll have to have the right attitude. When you're HIV-positive, it helps to be positive, so you stay healthy...uh, do I look healthy to you?"

I thought tha questions was s'pose ta be about me. But he knew I was gonna bite. "Yeah, you do."

"Well, looks can be deceiving."

I just stared at him. "You mean…"

"Yes. I'm HIV-positive."

I ain't know what ta say. And so I said what folks usually say when someone tells them some bad news that really ain't got nuthin ta do wit' them… "I…I'm sorry, man."

"Why are you sorry? It isn't your fault."

I shrugged.

"I was one of those folks who thought AIDS looked like some of the people in the ads on these walls. Frail. Emaciated. Almost skeletal. And I didn't think you had to have safer sex all the time if you were with someone you loved."

"I thought it was called safe sex?"

"Well, as me and many other people know, there is nothing safe about sex. In fact, there is nothing in this life that is safe—and that includes loving someone."

He knocked me over wit' that one. Bein in love, I could feel him. It's some cray-zee, scary shit. "*Day-um*, brotha. *That's* deep."

"Yes, it is."

Since he opened that do', I decided ta walk right on thru it. "Uh…how long you known?"

"I'm the one who is supposed to be asking the questions here, remember?" He smiled.

I smiled, too.

"I've known for twelve years."

"*Twelve* years?"

"Yes. You sound surprised."

"Yeah, I am, kinda."

"Well, with all the research and new treatments, people are living longer. I feel…fine. And I want to stay that way. I guess you could say I'm holding out for a cure. I mean, it'd be cruel to come this far and die. People think that AIDS is a death sentence, and for some it has been. But it's only a death sentence for those who believe it is."

"Uh…I guess I was one of them people who thought that."

"You said, 'thought.' Does that mean you no longer think that?"

"Nah, I don't."

He smiled. "Good."

"Uh…can I ask another question?"

"Sure."

"Was you s'pose ta tell me about you?"

"Well…no. But I think it's important for folks who walk up in here to know that it does happen to us. And it's hard to believe it still can't when it's sitting across the table from you."

I nodded in agreement. "Yeah, it is."

"So, do you have any other questions you want to ask about me or anything else we've talked about so far?"

"Nah. I don't think so."

"Well, I have one for you."

"What?"

"Are you afraid of needles?"

"Nah, I ain't."

"Good. It'll pinch, it'll smart, but it won't hurt."

"No prob."

"OK."

"Uh, thanks a lot, brotha."

"For what?"

"Fuh bein so up front wit' me."

"Well, somebody's gotta be. Too many of us have been too silent for too long. Just don't tell anybody I told you, OK?"

"Yo, ya secret is safe wit' me."

"And so are yours."

He finished up by tellin me about other diseases folks get but are almost never talked about cuz AIDS been gettin all tha press lately. (I ain't know syphilis was on tha rise, and I ain't never heard of hepatitis C, which can incubate fuh *twenty* years inside of you and you not even know it.) Then he brought me ta tha test room. I held out my hand ta shake his and thanked him again. It wasn't until I was on my way back ta New York that I freaked. I mean, even I know ya can't get AIDS from shakin somebody's hand. But knowin I did it…it was just a little too close fuh comfort, ya know what I'm sayin?

But I prob'ly done shook tha hands of a whole lota folks who are positive or got AIDS and didn't know it. So I give tha brotha much props: He ain't hafta tell me nuthin, but he did—and I'm glad he did. Knowin about Eazy made me wanna take tha test, but meetin someone like him that I could reach out and touch wit' it…that does make a world of diff'rence. So what if I felt a little uneasy? He was helpin me, and I appreciated that. I hope my bein open made him feel jood. I wasn't takin no pity on him. I guess I just hoped that, if I was in his shoes, somebody would do tha same ta me.

So *this* is what it feels like ta be a star.

Me, Little Bit, Troy, and Thomas Grayson a.k.a. Tommy Boy (who became President of Image Relations at All-American two months ago cuz of tha big splash I made) was waitin in tha wings of tha office of Gary Bloom, Macy's Men's Apparel Manager. I was makin my first appearance there as a A-A model. Now, we expected there ta be a crowd, maybe a hundred folks. Macy's was bankin on all them white girls who read *Seventeen* and bought A-A garb fuh they boyfriends ta come out. But we ain't expect there ta be this mass of folks standin outside, tryin ta get in. Traffic cops had ta be called in ta control thangz. And while there was some color up in that crowd, I saw so many white faces I just knew somebody else had ta be signin autographs.

What can I say? Tha Kid got mass appeal.

But I know Tommy Boy and Gary was nervous as hell—and it wasn't becuz they wasn't prepared fuh so many folks showin up or that thangz almost got outa hand when somebody mistakenly told some girls in tha crowd that they spotted me near tha perfume/cologne department (there was almost a near riot).

I wasn't gonna do it. Yeah, tha pay was jood (twenty g's, G). Tha hours was jood (well, it was only fuh an hour). And tha work itself would be a breeze (just sittin at a table, signin 'zines and pics of myself, and prob'ly takin a few photos here 'n' there). But not three days after they announced me comin ta tha store, they dissed me. Well, *they* didn't; one of their employees did. And it happened right in fronta Li'l Brotha Man.

We wanted ta buy Little Bit a new TV set. He had his 19-inch fuh so long (nine years) that its color was shot (ev'rybody looked orange). He ain't want one of dem giant-screen jammies like mine (not that he really had tha room fuh one). So when I saw that monster sale advertised on TV, I knew we had ta get him one. It wasn't his birthday and it was two weeks befo' Valentine's Day, but ain't none of that matter. It don't hafta be no holiday fuh me ta buy my Baby a present. Ev'ry day wit' him is a special occasion.

Anyway, L'il Brotha Man picked one out, and I went searchin fuh a salesperson when this white woman—she reminded me of Sharon Stone (if Sharon Stone was brunette, flat-chested, and anorexic)—just popped up outa nowhere.

"Can I help you?" she asked in that tone white folks use when they tryin ta be polite, but they really wish you'd just disappear. She was smackin gum.

"Yes, we want one of these, please," answered L'il Brotha Man, who was pointin ta it.

"Oh, do you?" She was lookin down at him as if he was a bug she was about ta squash. "Do you have enough money?"

Now, I knew that was fuh me. I guess I ain't look like I could buy it—if a brotha is dressed like a hood (baggy jeans, boots, cap), ain't no way he can—and if he can, we know where he got them funds from, right? But we know it wouldn'ta made no diff'rence if I fell up in tha place wearin a suit and tie. So, since she was hell-bent on fuckin wit' me, I was gonna fuck wit' her. "Yeah. He got enuff money ta buy it—and pay yo' salary fuh a year." I laughed.

She ain't find that funny. "That's a joke?"

I wanted so bad ta say, "No, *you* tha joke, bitch," but held my tongue. "It's a inside joke. Right, Li'l Brotha Man?" I winked at him.

He just went along wit' me. "Right, Daddy," he grinned.

"I see," she grunted, not at all amused. "Uh, if you'd

like to purchase it, I can take care of you over here."

She hadn't even finished that sentence when she started walkin off. Even Li'l Brotha Man looked at her like she was buggin. We followed her.

"Will that be cash or credit?" She said it wit'out even lookin up from some booklet she was flippin thru.

"Neither."

Now she looked up. "Uh, we don't accept money orders."

"I don't have a money order."

"We don't accept personal checks."

"I don't have a personal check."

"And we don't accept traveler's checks."

"Don't have none of them, either."

Tryin ta keep up wit' our convo, Li'l Brotha Man's head was goin back 'n' forth like he was watchin a Ping-Pong ball game or tennis match.

She was truly put out. She huffed. "Well then, how do you propose to pay for this item?"

I went in my pocket and drew it out. I smiled. "I never leave home wit'out it."

Yeah, it was my Am Ex.

Frustrated, she put her right hand on her hip. "I *asked* you if it would be cash or credit."

I leaned on tha counter. "I know. That's a *charge* card. There's a diff'rence."

She sho' didn't appreciate bein schooled by a nigger; she had that How *dare* you frown. "Do you have identification?"

I took out my driver's license.

She looked at it. She looked at me. "Do you have something else?"

"Why you need sumthin else?"

"We need *two* pieces of identification to make the transaction."

I knew that was a lie. If I didn't have a driver's license, *maybe*. But I went along. I took out my passport. I usually carry it wit' me when I'm on da road cuz sometimes a state ID ain't enuff fuh some folks. Sumthin told me ta carry it wit' me.

And, apparently, this still wasn't enuff fuh her. "We can't accept that."

"Why not?"

"Because, it isn't an acceptable form of identification."

"Accordin ta who?"

"According to store policy," she snapped.

I looked at a glass partition that was between me and tha cash register. "Well, this *store policy* posted right here don't say *nuthin* about not acceptin a passport."

She arched her head ta read it (like she didn't know what tha fuck it said). I guess she didn't think *I* knew how ta read. She knew she had no choice but ta accept it.

She swiped my card. That confirmation came thru just like that (ta her su'prise) and a receipt popped up. She laid it down on tha counter fuh me ta sign. I did. She compared tha signatures fuh like 10 seconds (she was just *so* disappointed ta find that I signed tha right name, that not a single curve or loop was diff'rent, and that them *i*'s was dotted). She punched them keys on tha register. She handed me my card and both receipts.

She pointed down tha hall. "You'll be able to collect your merchandise over there." I felt like bitin off her hand; she had it just a inch away from my face. She then turned her back.

No "Thank you for shopping with us."

No "Have a nice day."

No "Please come again."

She may as well said "Fuck you."

I was gonna let this bitch have it. "Well, I won't be collectin it."

She turned her head, annoyed that I was still there. "Uh, you want it delivered? I *wish* you would have told me…"

She sumthin else, ain't she?

"No, I don't want it delivered. In fact, I don't want it."

She turned completely around. "What?"

I held out my card and both receipts. I smiled. "I'd like a refund, please."

"*Excuse me?*" She was really beside herself now.

"*And* I wanna see yo' supervisor." I looked at that name-tag pinned on her blouse fuh tha first time. "*Doris.*"

Just my luck, her supervisor happened ta be comin our way. She was a sista. I don't know if she heard our exchange, but she could tell by tha looks on both of our faces that neither one of us was pleased.

"Is there a problem?" she asked, approachin us.

"Yeah," I smirked. "You hired it." I shot Doris a look. Doris rolled her eyes. I wanted ta knock 'em outa her head.

"I'm sorry, sir?" She was puzzled.

"*Doris* don't seem to know much about customer service. And, if she do, she must reserve it fuh yo' white customers."

That I would even go there made Doris steam. She turned a whiter shade of pale.

"Uh, you..." Tha sista was lookin at me funny. It clicked. "Uh, aren't you the model? I'm sorry, I don't remember your name."

"Raheim Rivers."

"Yes, Mr. Rivers, it's *great* to meet you." She held out her hand. We shook. "I'm Charisse Dawes, the assistant manager of the electronics department." She glared at Doris. "Mr. Rivers will be *appearing* here next month as part of our models signing series."

Doris's face *cracked*.

Charisse tried her best ta clean shit up. "I'm so sorry that the service wasn't up to your standards. May I help you?"

She knew that it was in her best int'rest not ta let me leave that store an unhappy customer—especially since I had been and would be bringin them a lota bizness via All-American. But I wasn't int'rested in makin nice. I just wanted ta get tha fuck outa there. "I just want my money back." I handed her my card and both receipts.

She gave Doris one of them We're gonna have a *serious* talk looks and did it. She tried ta engage me—"Are you sure I can't show you something else? We are so looking forward to your visit next month. All-American is one of the most popular designer names in our store"— and, ta Li'l Brotha Man—"This cute little boy *has* to be your son. Are you a model like your daddy?"—but I wasn't in tha mood.

Befo' we left, she gave me her business card and was really accomodatin and apologetic. "Please do come back. I would be more than happy to wait on you. I hope that this one shopping experience won't cloud your view of us."

She knew it would.

Now, Li'l Brotha Man watched this whole thang wit' bugged eyes. He knew his daddy did all that fuh a reason. And he figured it out.

"Daddy?" he asked when we was on our way home.

"Yeah?"

"Um…did that lady, Doris, treat us like that because we Black?"

I nodded. "Yeah, my man. She did."

"Oh," he sighed.

It was one thing fuh *me* ta hafta deal wit' it; it's another fuh my son ta. That look on his face… He was shocked. Bewildered. Hurt. I could see his pain. I could feel his pain. That's a look I ain't never wanna see. And it made me so fuckin angry ta know that, while it mighta been tha first time he experienced some shit like that, it *wouldn't* be tha last. A tear came outa my right eye and started ta slowly roll down my face.

He rubbed my right hand wit' his left. "Daddy, why are you crying?"

"Um…" I really didn't know what ta say. "Don't worry about it, my man."

"It's not your fault," he consoled, peerin at me wit'

them concerned eyes and wipin that tear.

"No, it's not. And it ain't yours, either." I kissed him on his forehead.

We knew whose fault it was, and so did Charisse. When I relayed tha story ta Troy and he called her up, he learned that Doris was placed on probation (ya really didn't think they was gonna fire her fuh treatin us tha way they believe we're s'pose ta be treated, didja?). When word got up ta Gary, he sent me a certified letter, apologizing fuh what he called an "unfortunate incident." And Macy's offered ta give me that TV set fuh free, as well as a gift certificate fuh $500 (y'all shellin out five figures fuh me ta appear there and think that measly old coupon is gonna make amends?).

When I refused both of them token gifts and told 'em I wasn't gonna do tha event, Tommy Boy flipped. A-A had never had a model do an event there befo', so he had a lot ridin on this. "Are you sure it was because you are black?" he questioned. "Maybe you misunderstood."

White folks kill me. Tha shit can be starin them right in the mutha-fuckin face and they still wanna pretend like it ain't there. And ain't it just like them ta try and shift tha focus on you, as if you don't know when you bein mistreated becuz of yo' skin color. I wasn't havin it. "Yo, she did ev'rything except follow me 'n' Li'l Brotha Man around tha store. And tha only reason why she ain't do *that* was becuz those TV sets are too big ta put in our pockets and just run out tha store wit'."

Like Tommy Boy, Troy wanted me ta do it—hell, he

wanted his cut—but he also knew that takin a stand like
this was much mo' important than spendin an hour wit'
some giggly high school girls. He believed I should do it
only if I felt they was comin correct. So, when a member of Macy's board of directors got wind of what happened (and I wonder how *he* found out), he had that
bitch fired and took time outa his own schedule ta come
ta one of my shoots ta personally apologize. That's when
I considered still doin it—but not wit'out talkin ta tha
man in charge first.

"So, whatcha think I should do?" I asked.

"That lady doesn't work there anymore?"

"No, she don't."

"And that man came all the way to D.C. to apologize?"

"He sho' nuff did."

He thought about it. "I think you should do it."

So, wit' Li'l Brotha Man's permission, I'm here.

"We'll start in a minute or so. Can I get you anything?"
asked Gary, who was just fallin all over himself. He was a
real lanky guy, a coupla inches taller than me, and had a
square face, big blue eyes, a nose so slim it was amazin
he could breathe thru it, and lips that had been inject-
ed wit' too much collagen (I see a *lot* of that on tha
model circuit). He's also been spendin too much time at
that tannin salon—looks like his skin is burnt. And he
had ta be a chocoholic: How else could ya explain all them
pics of brothas all over his office? There wasn't a single shot
of a white boy ta be found, except tha one of himself and
a mugly (uh-huh, mo' ugly) muscle-bound brotha wit'

dred–locs on his desk.

"Nah, I'm cool," I said, sittin back in tha brown leather recliner behind his desk.

"Are you sure?"

"Yeah."

"Alright. I'll be right back." He walked outa tha office. Tommy Boy followed, closin tha do' behind him. I guess they was gonna compare notes.

Just like me, Little Bit, 'n' Troy.

"Hmph…no wonder he worked so hard to get you in here," said Troy, lookin around. "He got you and almost every other Black man who ever modeled decoratin these walls: Rashid Silvera, Ben Lawson, Jhamil Henderson, Bill Hammond, James Vest, Alan Cephus, Ty Spears. Even Billy Dee and Michael Jordan."

"I guess there's no question what flavor *he* prefers," added Little Bit.

I nodded. "Ha, no doubt."

"So, are you ready?" asked Little Bit.

"Yeah, I'm ready."

"Are you nervous?"

"Nah. Why should I be?"

"Well, it's not that you should be. But I haven't seen a commotion like this since I made the mistake of going to Tower Records the day R.E.M. made an appearance."

Gary 'n' Tommy Boy popped back in.

"We're ready if you are," Gary announced.

I got up. "Let's do this."

They had a part of tha men's sportswear department

sectioned off. There was a big desk draped wit' a large American flag, and a black canopy as long and tall as a billboard stood behind it wit' blowups of seven of my A-A poses: me in red/white/blue briefs; me in red/white/blue boxers; me in blue jeans wit' a handkerchief hangin outa my back pocket like Bruce Springsteen; me in light blue overalls and a straw hat, sittin on bales of hay in a barn; me in khakis, a cotton shirt, a brown sweater tied around my waist, and sportin gold horn-rimmed glasses (yeah, that studious look); me in my golf gear—lime-green polyester pants and a yellow shirt; and me in my ski gear—parka, boots, knit cap, goggles, and gloves, all in black 'n' gray. They also had copies of each photo on tha table fuh folks who might not have a 'zine or other item fuh me ta sign.

Folks was s'pose ta be in a single line, but you know ya can't make a crowd like that do thangz wit' some order. When a few people spotted me, there was a lota screamin and shoutin: *"It's him!" "Hi, Raheim!" "I love you!"* and "We love you!"

"Ha, move over New Kids on the Block: Here is *the* new kid on the block!" joked Little Bit, pokin me in tha side.

As I sat down, I waved at tha crowd. You could *hear* them hearts swoon.

Gary stepped up ta a mic that was off ta my left. He tapped it. "Hello. Hello, everyone." He waited fuh folks ta quiet down. "Thank you. I'm Gary Bloom, the Manager of Men's Apparel here at Macy's, and on behalf of our store and All-American, we would like to thank you for coming out today and welcoming one of the hottest models in the industry, Raheim Rivers." He nodded at me; I returned it. He had ta wait fuh tha hoots and hollers ta go down again. "We'd like to make this event as enjoyable as possible. So please, if you have something you'd like Mr. Rivers to sign, have it ready. If you'd like your picture taken with Mr. Rivers, you may walk around the table. But given the amount of time, he will not be able to rise out of his seat. Also, please refrain from taking more than two of the photos available on the table. We'd like to make sure that everyone who wants one can get one. And please be considerate and try not to take up too much time with him. There are many others waiting for their chance. Thank you."

And, wit' that, I went on ta sign 116 posters (tha one A-A came out wit' last year that's still sellin like crayzee), 92 photos, 112 magazines, and took 68 pictures (yeah, I kept a count). A few of them had posters that they musta swiped from bus stations. One took a picture of that Michelob billboard and had it blown up. Another had a collage of all my diff'rent pics. One girl wanted me ta sign her breast; another her belly (I signed their arms instead). One had an image of me tattooed on tha back of her left thigh. Two girls claimed they designed a Web page in my honor, wit' a link ta All-American's site. And a whole troop of 'em introduced themselves as members of my fan club. Now, that *really* tripped me out. I got a fan club and didn't know it. They gave me a packet of info about their group.

And, then there was all those cards and gifts—most of 'em jewelry boxes, but a few were larger yet compact enuff ta hold in one hand. It blew me away that folks would think that much of me, a total stranger, just a face they see, and give me presents. I wish I coulda opened 'em all up right there, just ta see tha looks on their faces, but there wasn't enuff time. So, I put 'em all ta tha side ta open later.

But there was a few familiar faces. Like Michelle, that receptionist from *Your World*, Little Bit's old job.

"Mister, if I had known I would have to go through all of *this* to get your John Hancock, I would've just sent my poster to Mitchell for you to sign," she declared, handin it ta me.

I took it. I chuckled. "Sorry." I signed.

"Ha, *I'm* the one whose sorry. I'll know next time that I had better be here at least an hour early. I knew you were all that, but I didn't know you were *all that!*"

We laughed.

"Thanks fuh ruffin it out." I gave it back ta her.

"Thanks for representin so well. Keep makin us proud." We smiled. She squeezed my hand. She blew me a kiss and went off ta converse wit' Little Bit.

And then there was Gene 'n' B.D., two of Little Bit's best friends.

"Y'all ain't hafta stand on no line," I said.

"*Tell* me about it," croaked Gene. He elbowed B.D. "But this one felt it was important we show our support, being surrounded for 45 minutes by a herd of trashy teen terrors all itchin to have their twats twiddled."

"Ha, they ain't the only ones," grinned B.D., who, even tho' he was wearin a big leather coat, couldn't hide that big booty. He was lookin at all them pics on tha table. He clutched his chest. "My, my, my, my, *my*...they all are so *fab*ulous, I don't know which one to pick."

"Well, you can take one of each. I can give ya a personal autograph fuh 'em later on."

"Mmm, I'll hold you to that." He winked.

I blushed. "Where Babyface at?"

"He's over there with Mitch," said Gene. He rolled his eyes. "*He* was smart enough to stand off to the side."

"Oh, will you stop complaining?" His photos in his right hand and his camera in his left, B.D. playfully started pushin Gene along. "You can tell your *great*-grandchildren that you were one of only *two* fags who had his picture taken with Raheim Rivers at his very first signing. Do you know how much a picture like that could be worth one day?"

I saw that lightbulb come on—and them dollar signs pop up in Gene's eyes. He eased himself behind tha desk, wrapped his arm around my shoulder, and cheezed it up, as B.D. took our pic. Then he returned tha favor, takin a pic of me 'n' B.D. (and, yeah, ya know I had ta pat B.D. on that azz).

It was jood ta see them. It was jood ta see Michelle. It was jood ta see ev'rybody. So, yeah, I was happy I changed my mind and did it. So was Gary (who said they sold 100 posters and just about all their A-A wares), Tommy Boy (who knew that such a successful event meant *mo' money, mo' money, mo' money* fuh All-American), and Troy (who had our check).

It was all over at 7:30. They shoulda given me mo' money fuh that overtime, cuz I was exhausted. Smilin all up in folks' faces, even when they was sayin stoopid-azz stuff like, "You're the most beautiful black man I've ever seen" and "Will you marry me?" It had been a week since I had been flashed so much and becuz of all that clickin, I was seein spots befo' my eyes. (I also had ta pose wit' Gary and Tommy Boy fuh some media shots; photogs from *The New York Daily News* and *Vibe* was there.) And becuz I had never written my name so many times in such a short period of time, my left hand, wrist, and arm was all tight.

Ya know tha Kid had worked up a serious appetite, so Tommy Boy took me—well, it was mo' like us—out fuh dinner. Little Bit, Troy, and Gary came along, as did B.D., Gene, Babyface, and Angel, who showed up when ev'rything was just about over (he had ta work late). Tommy Boy, Troy, and Gary rode in Tommy Boy's BMW, while ev'rybody else piled inta my limo (provided by Macy's). This time, we had down home, Downtown: The Pink Tea Cup. You know Tommy Boy and Gary ate it all up, bein in tha midst of all that Blackness. Turned out that B.D. and Gary knew each other; Gary had once dated a dancer in his troupe. Gene was bein really touchy-feely wit' Angel, who ain't seem ta mind; I know they had met when we gave Little Bit a su'prise birthday party last year, but I ain't know sumthin had happened between 'em (ya know I had ta get tha lowdown on *that* later on). Babyface and Troy finally met after talkin on tha phone so many times. Babyface ain't my lawyer—I don't have him on payroll. I guess you'd call him my legal advisor. He's been a big help explainin all that legalese and makin sure that whatever deal I sign is on tha up-n-ups, includin my agreement wit' Troy. And, while he always say he don't mind doin it fuh free, I still give him a li'l sumthin sumthin.

After three hours of gabbin, grubbin, and givin that jukebox a lota coins, we left just after 11. I signed a pic fuh tha restaurant so they could put it on their Wall of Fame. Me 'n' Little Bit had tha limo take us ta his place in Brooklyn. After he massaged my fingers, hands, and arms wit' oil (he knew just what ta do), we got in bed and I opened up my cards (mainly "Good Luck in Your Career") and gifts (Africentric and American-flagged bracelets, necklaces, anklets, scarves, handkerchiefs, and hats). I saved tha prettiest box—glittery gold wit' a light green bow—fuh last.

I read tha note first:"I hope the scent will lead you to me."

Like me, Little Bit figured it was gonna be some cologne. But it wasn't.

I pulled tha tissue paper back, and there was a pink pair of women's lace panties.

Me 'n' Little Bit looked at each other—and then laughed so hard we cried.

I remember readin about shit like this happenin ta Marvin Gaye, Teddy Pendergrass, Barry White, Peabo Bryson, even Michael Jackson (way back in da day). But *me?*

There was a glittery gold business card taped ta them. It had MONA printed on it, and *all* her digits—home, work, fax, beeper, pager, *and* cell.

Little Bit just shook his head in amazement. "Well, if *this* isn't a sign that you've arrived, I don't know what is!"

Money makes people act funny.

Now, I expected ta have niggaz I ain't hung wit' in years and relatives I ain't never seen or knew existed (and, yeah, they turned out *not* to be family at all) come outa tha woodwork. And I wasn't one bit su'prised when one female from around da way claimed her baby was mine (even her own mama, who is a crackhead, could see that, as dark as we both was, ain't no way we could make a high-yella, green-eyed kid wit' red hair).

But I ain't *never* expect it from my own son.

After I had picked Li'l Brotha Man up from school, we

went ta his dentist's appointment—and, like his daddy, he don't have a single cavity. We was on our way home when...

"Daddy?"

"Yeah, my man?"

"Um...may I have a allowance?"

"Hunh?"

"Can I have a allowance?"

"A allowance?"

"Yes."

"Ha, do you even know what a allowance is?"

"Uh-huh."

I couldn't wait ta hear this. "A'ight. I'm list'nin."

"A allowance is money you get each week from your mommy and daddy."

"Ah. And why you want one?"

"Because, I do."

I frowned. "Now, what I told you about that?"

"What, Daddy?"

"You know what. You just don't want sumthin or wanna do sumthin just becuz you do. There's always a reason why. So give it up."

"I...I just want one, Daddy."

"That ain't it, and you know it."

He looked down. "I...I want one because... because... my friends have one."

"What friends?"

"Um...Corey, Tiffany, and Joey."

"Uh-huh. So if Corey, Tiffany, and Joey was gonna cut school, you gonna do that, too?"

He lifted his head and looked at me. "That's different, Daddy."

"What's so diff'rent about it? You followin tha crowd, and what I tell you about wantin ta do what ev'rybody else do?"

"I…I don't know."

"You do too know, Li'l Brotha Man. What I say?"

"You…you said…you said I have to follow my own lead."

"Right. But is that what you doin by wantin sumthin they got?"

"I guess not."

"You *know* not."

"But, Daddy, you can afford to give me one."

"I can? How you know that?"

"Because, you told me you make almost 10 times as much as you did before. And I did the math."

"You did, hunh?"

"Uh-huh. If you were making $29,000, that means you're making almost *$290,000!* That makes you rich!"

"I ain't rich, Li'l Brotha Man, and I hope you ain't been goin 'round tellin people that, is you?"

"No. You told me, never tell anybody how much money you or Mommy make because it's none of their business."

"Jood."

"But it's still a lot of money, Daddy."

"No, it ain't."

"But you almost a millionaire."

"*Almost* is a big word, my man. I'm just earnin a livin."

"What do you mean, Daddy?"

"What I mean is that I mighta made that much in tha past year, but I ain't have it all at one time. It's been comin a little bit at a time. Besides, Black men don't get ta be rich in America like white folks."

"But what about Michael Jackson, Daddy?"

"Li'l Brotha Man, there's only one Michael Jackson in this world. There ain't many brothas breakin tha bank like him."

"So, what do you call somebody that makes as much money as you?"

Jood question. I had ta think on that one. "Uh…you could call 'em well-off."

"Well-off?"

"Yeah. That's whatcha Daddy is gettin ta be. See, people think that you make that kinda money and you livin large, that you got it made. But I'm workin *hard* fuh tha money. Tha money ain't workin fuh me like it does fuh rich folks. They don't have no 9-to-5 job where they gotta punch a time clock; all they gotta do is sit back and count their green. I can't do that. I got a lota responsibilities, bills ta pay. You know I gotta pay my agent. You remember how much he get?"

"Twenty percent."

Cuz Troy was doin such a jood job, we doubled his take after I was wit' him three months—and he been provin he's worth it ever since. "Right. And I gotta pay my taxes next week."

"You mean, to Uncle Sam, Daddy?"

"Yeah. And then I gotta take care of tha folks in my life, and that's you, Grammy, Sunshine, and Lit…Mitchell." *Woof*…I had ta catch myself.

He started thinkin real hard about what I said. (Yup, tha tip of his left thumb went inta his mouth.) "Oh. So are you saying you can't afford to give me a allowance?"

"Nah, I ain't sayin that. What I'm sayin is that you can't be thinkin I can just give you sumthin cuz you want it or cuz yo' friends got it or cuz you think I got it like that. Now, if you had come ta me and said you wanted it so you could learn how ta handle money and see fuh yo'self whatcha Daddy goes thru, tryin ta budget and make sure ta spend it right, I mighta said yeah."

"You would?"

"Yeah, I would. I mean, you need ta learn tha value of money. And I guess gettin some kinda allowance would be a jood way ta do it. But you too young."

"No, I'm not," he protested.

"You don't think so?"

"No. I'm 6 years old. I'm a big boy, Daddy."

"Oh, you are, hunh?"

"Uh-huh. I can be responsible."

"You can, hunh?"

"Yes."

"A'ight, a'ight. I'll give you one."

His whole face lit up. "You will?"

"Yeah. But you gonna hafta take this seriously. You can't be spendin it all in one place, and you gotta save some of it."

"You mean, you want me to open a bank account?"

"You don't hafta, cuz I already did fuh ya."

"You did?"

"Yeah. I been savin a little ev'ry week since you been born. Now you can start puttin yo' own change in there, too."

"How much is in it, Daddy?"

"Don't worry about it. You ain't gonna see none of it until you goin off ta college."

"Can I put my allowance in my own bank at home?"

"You got a bank at home?"

"Yes, my piggy bank."

"Ah. What kinda bank is it?"

"Oscar the Grouch. Uncle D gave it to me for my birthday, remember?"

Oh, yeah. He did. "Anything in that bank?"

"Uh-huh. I put the pennies I find around the house, in school, and in the streets in there."

"Well, you gonna hafta start puttin some nickels 'n' dimes in that piggy bank ev'ry week."

"How much you gonna give me, Daddy?"

"How much you think you can handle?"

"I don't know. I guess five dollars."

I almost jumped outa my skin. *Five dollars? A week?*

"Yes."

"Man, whatcha gonna do wit' all that money?"

"I don't know. Spend some and save some, like you told me."

"Li'l Brotha Man, that's a bit too much fuh you ta have. I ain't get nuthin like that 'til I was 12."

"But Corey gets that much each week—"

"Well, I ain't int'rested in what Corey or any of yo' other friends be gettin, and you shouldn't be, either. We talkin about you, not them. I ain't givin you no allowance so you can compete wit' them. We doin it so you learn a lesson, remember?"

"Yes."

"A'ight, then. I think we can give you a dollar a week."

"*One dollar?*"

"Yeah."

"Aw, come *on*, Daddy."

"A'ight, where we goin, lemme know, now…"

"This is the '90s."

I chuckled. "Oh, it is?"

"Yes. That's not gonna be enough."

"Not enuff fuh what? Man, it ain't like you gonna have a lota stuff ta do wit' tha money. Me 'n' Sunshine take care of ev'rything you need, any-ol'-way. And how you sound? You tellin *me*, tha man wit' tha coins, what's not enuff fuh *you*?"

"Make it four, Daddy."

"No."

"Three?"

"No."

"Please?"

"No."

"*Pleeze?*"

"Why?"

"Because I can spend $1.50, and then I can save $1.50."

"Hmph, you just got this all figured out, don't cha?"
He showed all them teeth.

I surrendered. "A'ight, a'ight. We'll make it three. But you only gettin it once ev'ry *two* weeks, and you gonna hafta save half ev'ry time you get it. How that sound?"

He nodded his approval. "That sounds jood."

"And I don't want you cryin about not havin no money. I ain't givin ya no extra loot, so ya better make it last."

"I will."

"And I want ya ta keep a log, a'ight?"

"A log, Daddy?"

"Yeah. Ev'ry week, write down how much you get, how much you put in yo' bank, and how much you got altogether."

"OK. I will."

"You real jood wit' that math, so I know you can keep that count. And you just ain't gettin sumthin fuh nuthin. You gotta keep them grades up. If they go down, so do yo' funds. And you gotta make sure you get no cavities. You got it?"

"Yes."

"And I don't want you worryin about what them folks at yo' school got or be gettin, you hear? Just cuz they get sumthin you don't, don't make them better than you. You remember that talk we had about you goin ta this school?"

"Yes. You said that I'm just as jood as anybody."

"Right. You got yo' own thang goin on, man, and you gotta be thankful fuh that. And if them friends wanna tell you all they bizness, let 'em. But don't be tellin nobody how much money you get."

"I won't, Daddy."

"A'ight then. Uh, you ask Sunshine about gettin a allowance?"

"Uh-huh. Mommy said to ask you. She said whatever you said was fine."

"Mmm…ain't it just like Sunshine ta give me sumthin like this ta handle," I mumbled.

"What did you say, Daddy?"

"Nuthin."

"Uh, Daddy, when will I start getting paid?"

"*Gettin paid?* Man, you ain't gettin paid cuz you ain't got no job, a'ight? You receivin a allowance. Tha magic word in there is allow. I'm *a-llow-in* you ta have this money cuz I trust you wit' it. You got that?"

"Yes."

I shrugged. "I guess you can start gettin it on Friday."

"OK. Daddy?"

"Yeah?"

"It's Friday."

"It is?"

"Yes."

"Ah, a'ight. I'll give it ta ya when we get ta tha house."

"OK. Daddy?"

"Yeah?"

"Thanks."

"You welcome, my man. Just keep makin us proud."

"I will. I'm gonna save so much money, I'll be able to give *you* a allowance!"

"Oh, yeah?"

He nodded. "Uh-huh."

"Just save enuff ta send yo'self ta college, a'ight?"

"So, whatcha think?"

Me 'n' Moms was on her balcony. Well, it wasn't her balcony yet, but I wanted it ta be.

She peeked over tha railin. "It's so high up."

"Ma, it's just tha eighth flo'. It ain't like you on tha top."

"How many floors are there again?"

"Sixteen."

"Well, you count that lobby and mezzanine level, and I'm closer to the top than the bottom."

"So, you wanna be below eight? That won't be no problem."

"No, no, that's OK. Hmph...a mezzanine. Makes me feel

like I'm in a hotel." She sucked her teeth. "Uh, you said that doorman is downstairs 24 hours, seven days a week?"

"Yeah."

"Do you know how they hire them?"

Here she go, fishin again fuh another excuse. "Nah. Why?"

"Francie told me about how some of these buildings get ripped off by the doormen. I hope they screen these people. For all we know, they could be paroled murderers and rapists."

"Ma, if it's gonna make you feet better, I'll ask about it, a'ight?"

"No, no, no, don't go to any trouble on my account."

"If it's gonna put yo' mind at ease, it ain't gonna be no trouble."

I could tell she was tryin ta find sumthin else ta nit-pick about. She finally did.

"You sure we still in Harlem?"

I shook my head, grinnin. "Yeah, Ma. Why?"

"Because I ain't never seen so many white folks in Harlem before."

"Ma, all you saw was five or six. That ain't a lot."

"If they ain't cops or firemen, then that's a lot."

"Ma, you said you don't wanna leave Harlem and you ain't. This just a side of Harlem you ain't seen."

"You can say that again." She sighed. She turned ta me. "You sure you can afford this?"

I knew she was gonna get around ta that, and I was ready fuh it. "Didn't I tell you not ta worry about it? I got it."

"I just don't want you goin out spendin all this money."

"I'm spendin it on who I wanna, a'ight?"

"Why don't you just concentrate on you? I can wait. You're gonna need that money to furnish your own apartment, and—"

"Ma, will you quit already? I wanna do this fuh you, a'ight?"

"I just don't want you goin broke."

"I ain't." And I won't be. I been puttin most of my money in tha bank: I got a checking, a money market, and three savings accounts (one of my own, one fuh Li'l Brotha Man, and one fuh Precious, Brotha Man's daughter), two CDs, a safe deposit box, and an IRA (like Little Bit says, ya just can't live fuh today, ya gotta plan fuh tha future). And I bought a few savings bonds and some stock in America Online, Microsoft, and All-American (hay, if I don't invest in myself…). I've never spent this much money at once, but this is a day-um jood deal. Becuz I'm gonna be payin fuh it up front wit' cash, they knockin 10% off that purchase price, slashin tha closin costs in half, and givin her a free parkin space (which I'm gonna be usin). And this apartment is gonna double in value in a few years, wit' all these so-called urban renewal projects goin on in tha community (of course, ya know they ain't buildin and fixin all this shit up fuh *our* benefit; we gonna be seein a whole lot mo' white folks in this area soon). So, if Moms still wants ta move down-South when she retires from her job, she can sell it, buy herself a house, and have a nice piece of change left over.

"Anyway," I continued ta argue, "it ain't like I been goin on shoppin sprees. And you been waitin too long ta have sumthin like this."

She smiled. "Yes. A de-luxe apartment, somewhat in the sky. I feel like Louise Jefferson."

We laughed.

She hugged herself. "The lobby is nice. That carpeting...I was tempted to kick off my shoes and walk on it. Those elevators are so damn quiet, it's like they're not movin. I love that kitchen: big cabinets, a dishwasher, and a refrigerator that makes ice cubes. That will come in handy. And that bathroom...I can get used to that jacuzzi. And that bedroom! I think you could fit two king-sized beds in there! And those walk-in-closets! I don't have enough clothes and shoes to fill up all that space!" She realized she was gettin excited; she caught herself.

I chuckled. "C'mon, Ma, don't even play that. You ain't foolin me. You love it."

She blushed.

"So when you wanna move in? All you gotta do is pick out what tile and carpet you want, and—"

She frowned. "Just because I love it doesn't mean I want to move in."

"Why not?"

"Because."

"Be-cuz?"

"Yes, because."

"C'mon, Ma, now you startin ta sound like Li'l Brotha Man."

Speakin of…

Knock-knock.

We both turned ta tha balcony do'. "Yeah?" I called out.

Li'l Brotha Man came outside. "So what do you think, Grammy?"

She smiled. "What do *you* think?"

"I like it, especially my bedroom. We can walk to Mommy's from here. It's just five blocks away. You can see the building from up here." He pointed ta it. "See, it's over there."

Moms put her right arm around him. "Yes, I see."

"But you can't see our windows. They in the front of the house. And Daddy's place is right around the corner!"

"Uh-huh. So, what do you think Grammy should do?" she asked.

He smiled. "I think you should sign on the dotted line."

"You do, hunh?"

"Yes, I do."

She looked at me. She pinched his cheek. "I think I will."

Li'l Brotha Man grinned. "Jood!" He ran back inside.

She watched him, grinnin. "I guess he's gonna love havin *three* bedrooms."

"Yeah."

She leaned on tha railin. She sighed.

"Ma, you knew you wanted ta move in when we pulled up in fronta tha place. Why was you holdin back?"

She looked at me. "I wasn't holdin back. It's just that… baby, when you've lived someplace for half your life, it's hard...to just say 'Yeah, it's time to move,' even if you want to."

"I know, Ma. You ain't tha only one movin."

"Yes, I know, but I raised my family...I raised you there. It won't be just an apartment I'm leavin, it'll be home. It's gonna be hard to leave. It's gonna be hard to leave behind." She shed a few tears. She looked out.

I took her hand. We smiled.

"I know it ain't gonna be easy, Ma. But it ain't like you movin 3,000 miles away. If you get homesick fuh tha old spot, you can always visit that neck of tha 'hood. Besides, you gonna have another family ta raise."

She glared at me. "Mmm-hmm. Don't you mean *help* raise?"

I chuckled. "Yeah."

"Uh-huh. I already raised one child, OK? Hmph, at least he doesn't throw a fit when I tell him to pick up his toys or eat his vegetables."

I shrugged.

She squeezed my hand. She kissed me on my left cheek. "Thanks, baby."

"Nah, thanks go out ta you, Ma. I wouldn't be where I am, I wouldn't be *who* I am wit'out ya."

She hugged herself. "Well...I guess I finally got my piece of the pie."

"Y*ello?*"

"*Yo, Raheim. It's me—Angel.*"

"*I know. Whazzup?*"

"*Nuthin. Just coolin. Yo, I got some news.*"

"*Yeah, I know. I saw on tha news that he died.*"

"*Nah, nah, man, it ain't about Eazy.*"

"*It ain't?*"

"*Nah. And I know you ain't gonna like hearin it.*"

"*If you know that, then why you callin me up ta tell me?*"

"*Cuz, man, this ain't sumthin you can just wave off.*"

"*A'ight, a'ight. I'm list'nin.*"

"*Uh, you sittin down?*"

"*Am I sittin down? Nigga, it ain't gonna make no diff'rence if I'm sittin down or not. Just tell me.*"

"*Well, a'ight. I just found out that...David...he...he about ta make his exit.*"

"*He about ta make his...man, what tha fuck you talkin 'bout?*"

"*You know. He dyin.*"

"*He dyin?*"

"*Yeah.*"

"*Nigga, how he gonna be dyin?*"

"*I just ran inta Trey. You know, he 'n' David was roommates when y'all was kickin it.*"

"*Yeah. I never liked that bitch. He was always in our shit.*"

"*Trey said David been sick fuh like a year now. He been in and outa tha hospital. He said he ain't got much time left.*"

"*Uh...so why he...never mind. You ain't even gotta say it.*"

"*Trey said he been tryin ta find you.*"

"*Me? Why?*"

"*Cuz he wanted ta make sure you knew about him. And David wants ta see you.*"

"*He wanna see me?*"

"*Yeah.*"

"*Why?*"

"*Man, I don't know. I'm just deliv'rin a message. But if he on his way out, I guess he wanna see you one last time.*"

Silence.

"*Yo, Raheim? You there?*"

"*Yeah, I'm here.*"

"*Oh, yeah. I should know by now that when I don't hear nuthin on yo' end, that means you done heard sumthin you* ain't wanna hear. Yo, can I ask you a question?"

"Go 'head."

"Is David…is he one of tha folks you was wit' and you ain't use no glove?"

"Nah, nah. We always did."

"You sure?"

"Yeah, nigga, I'm sure. I should know, I fucked him."

"Just askin, man, sorry. Uh, you gonna go see him?"

"I…I don't know."

"Brotha, you should go see him."

"Why? It ain't gonna do no jood. It ain't gonna help him."

"Man, you don't know. It might."

"Man, if he dyin, seein me ain't gonna keep him alive."

"It ain't gonna keep him alive, but at least he'll get ta see you one last time. You know how he felt about you. He might have some things ta say ta you."

"Yeah, like how he hates Little Bit and how I'm gonna be so miserable wit' out his ass, right?"

"C'mon, man, he dyin. Why would he say some shit like that?"

"Cuz he always said shit like that, and dyin ain't gonna change him."

"How you know unless you go see him?"

"I ain't goin."

"Man, if you don't go cuz he wants ta see ya, you should go fuh you."

"Fuh me?"

"Yeah. You might not feel nuthin fuh him now, but when he dies you might come ta regret not goin and you'll be carryin around that guilt fuh tha rest of yo' life."

"Man, who tha fuck you s'pose ta be, Dr. Alvin Poussaint and shit? Tha only regrets I got is flauntin him up in Little Bit's face and goin back ta him fuh some when me 'n' Little Bit was fightin. I cut that tie, and I ain't gonna have no regrets cuz he ain't got no right ta be askin me fuh nuthin."

"Ice, brotha. Nuthin but ice, if ya ask me."

"Nigga, ain't no-fuckin-body ask you, a'ight? And what tha fuck is up wit' you? Ev'ry time you call me, you got bad news and shit."

"Yo, man, you think I like deliv'rin messages like this. I just thought you should know."

"Well, I ain't need ta know that. Here I am, waitin fuh my results, and you just tackin mo' shit on me."

"Yo, man, I'm sorry. I'm just tryin ta look out fuh yo' ass. But I keep my mouth shut from now on. But just in case you change yo' mind, he at Lady of Mercy in Boogie Down. Visitin hours are 12 ta 8."

Click.

"Yo, Mista All-American, can I have ya autograph?"

Me 'n' Angel went ta this party at Joey's, a hip-hop club in midtown, fuh Da Brat, celebratin her bein tha first female rapper ta go platinum. (Yeah, he hung up on me, but I guess I deserved it; as usual, I was takin shit out on him.) I guess that's one of tha great thangz about bein a celeb: gettin ta go ta all tha jamz. But I ain't had much time ta go ta many. In fact, this was only my second one; me 'n' Little Bit went ta tha list'nin party fuh Mary J. Blige's *My Life*. After we got some drinks and found a table ta sit at, Angel left me ta go mingle—and, I'm sure, find somebody ta tingle (there was nuthin but boom-bastic brothaz up in da place). I figured no one would recognize me in a room full of folks like L.L. Cool J, Queen Latifah, Kool Moe Dee, Salt 'N' Pepa wit' Spin, Left-Eye of TLC, and NBN's Treach (I had gotten all *their* autographs at Mary's bash).

But then came that query, and I was fuh a moment kinda flattered. Then I turned and saw who it was: Marion Lavelle Gaylord, aka Malice. (As he told me, wit' a given name like that, you'd *hafta* come up wit' sumthin tuff). Born and raised and still livin in Compton, he's 27 and is a R-rated version of Luther "2 Live Crew" Campbell. It's goin on two years, but he still has tha biggest rap record in tha industry. His debut, *Malice in Wonderland*, is still in tha top 10 and done charted five singles: "Three-hundred Sexty-Five Dayz A Year" (cour-tesy of Lady T's "365"), "Bootay Bandit," "Dr. Freakenstein" (which samples Patrice Rushen's "Feels So Real"), "Juicy Fruit" (yeah, he lifted that Mtume track), and "U A Ho (Don't Cha Know?)." He's one of tha acts that would be on C. Delores Tucker's hit list fuh offen-sive, degradin, sexist lyrics. We met in La La Land when I was out there filmin *Rebound*. He was producin a few tracks fuh its soundtrack and was visitin tha set one day. He came ev'ry day thereafter, offerin ta show me around tha city and hang out wit' him and his crew, takin me out ta dinner, and buyin me gifts (Air Jordans, a Rolex, a bracelet, and a fat, *not* phat, gold chain wit' my initials on it) I ain't accept.

Yeah, tha brotha was mackin me sumthin fierce. And I'd be lyin if I said I ain't enjoy it. I always wondered what it would be like ta kick it wit' a nigga in hip-hop. And do he know how ta *kick* it: He's tha one I messed around wit'. But it was a *whole* lota messin around and, as Angel guessed, it was *messy*: pullin here, tuggin there, grabbin this, squeezin that, wigglin 'n' wrestlin, gropin 'n' grindin, bumpin 'n' humpin, slippin 'n' slidin, lappin 'n' slappin, slurpin 'n' slammin, spankin 'n' yankin, smackin 'n' whackin, jerkin 'n' jogglin, nibblin 'n' gnawin, tastin 'n' bastin, tossin 'n' tonguin, eatin 'n' teasin, bobbin 'n' bangin, blowin 'n' *mowin*—chowin but *no* plowin, suckin but *no* pluckin, lickin but *no* stickin. It was so tense, so intense; it was so fuckin juicy, so fuckin funky, so fuckin jood. How fuckin jood was it? It was so fuckin jood that we just didn't break tha headboard ta tha bed—we broke it *down* (I'm lucky them folks bankin *Rebound* didn't charge me fuh it; they just accepted that my weight was too much fuh it and it gave out). Yeah, we *Rocked* (uh-huh, wit' a c-a-p-i-t-a-l R) da Casbah, drippin 'n' droppin loads all over ourselves, all over each other, all over my hotel room. And whoever was on either side of that room (and prob'-ly tha flo' above and tha one below) got mo' than a earful fuh like five hours straight. We was *loud*. Shit, nigga freaked my body so jood—from tha top of my head ta tha bottom of my feet and ev'ry spot and space in between— there was some sounds that came outa me I ain't never heard befo'. I got ta see up close and personal that all that braggin 'n' boastin he do in them songs ain't just a lota braggin 'n' boastin. Yup, he *is* Dr. Freakenstein.

He sexed me up. He sexed me down. He sexed me *all around*.

I know, I know, I *know*: How could I even go there, right? Yeah, you know I love Little Bit, that I'm still *in* love wit' Little Bit, and there ain't no other person I wanna be wit'. But…what can I say? I got weak. Shit, you woulda got weak too wit' a phyne-azz mutha-fucka like him—6 foot 2, 265 diesel-cut pounds, curly black hair, goatee, creamy caramel skin, hazy hazel eyes, delicious DSLs, stacked in da back and packin in da front—all up in yo' face. I know I crossed *that* boundary tha moment we kissed, but at least I stopped it befo' he took a dive inside of me—even tho' that, too, is a cop-out since we did just about ev'rythang *except* knock da boots. And I know many done claimed it, but I really was drunk; he was helpin me celebrate finishin tha shoot, and I made tha mistake of havin three very potent rum and Cokes. But, of course, *that* ain't no excuse either since I was conscious enuff ta initiate a lot of tha shit we did (he made tha first move, but I followed up wit' tha second and third).

Seein him made all that guilt I felt about doin what I did wit' him come back—and it also made me angry again. No, I wasn't angry at him fuh what happened between us; how could I be when I was a *very* willin participant? I was angry becuz of tha shit he pulled my last nite in La La Land. So I truly wasn't feelin seein him. And he could tell.

"Hay," I grumbled.

"Well, day-um, nigga, don't act so happy ta see me." He sat down next ta me. "So, whazzup?"

"Nuthin."

"You lyin."

"I'm lyin?"

"Yeah, you lyin, cuz a nigga like you who got it goin on always got sumthin goin on." He flashed them gold teeth.

"Is that right?"

"You know it is. I hear you gonna do that *Posse* flick and that hip-hop video show."

Day-um, how he hear about all of that shit? We ain't even sign papers fuh tha TV show yet, and I just gave them *Posse* folks a yes on Thursday.

He grinned. "I take it by that look on yo' face you must be wonderin how I know all this, hunh? Well, nigga, I told you I'd be keepin tabs on yo' phyne azz. Besides, I'm gonna be contributin a track ta that *Posse* soundtrack, too. Guess we just a travelin pair, ain't we?"

I shrugged. "I suppose."

"Ya know I'm gonna hafta be yo' first guest, G. It'd look funny if I ain't. Folks gonna wonder."

"I'll see what I can do."

"You do that."

"So, whazzup wit' you?"

"Man, you know, what can I say? Same shit, diff'rent toilet."

"Uh-huh. And whose toilet *you* been shittin in lately?" I smiled.

He didn't. "Funny."

"What you doin in da Big Apple?"

"Some session work. A new Cat named Dawg. I came ta tha party wit' him. After we get thru in tha studio, I'm gonna chill fuh a few days befo' I head back ta 90211. Speakin of which, ain't you s'pose ta be on yo' break?"

"Yeah, I am."

"Man, this ain't how you chill. You s'pose ta be off someplace, lyin low on some tropical island, kickin up that sand, and sippin on some tall, cool, juicy island mutha-fucka." He chuckled.

"Uh-huh. I wasn't plannin on comin, but my boy, Angel, he wanted ta. He all inta Da Brat, so he wanted ta meet her."

"Where this nigga at?"

"Off somewhere, tryin ta get some."

"Ah. Just like me." He grabbed his dick.

"Uh-huh. Any-ol'-way."

"Oh, yeah, you know we *can* do it any-ol'-way."

I shook my head. "You one cray-zee mutha-fucka."

"Cray-zee about some thangz." He looked around. "So, where this bitch at? We been waitin on her fuh almost a hour now."

"Somebody said she stuck in traffic somewhere."

"Bullshit. We don't know shit about time. Niggaz always gotta make a entrance and shit."

"Ha, like *you* don't do it? You be showin up two hours late fuh a concert, and then be gettin a serious a-ti-ma-tude cuz don't nobody wanna throw they hands in tha air."

"Yo, I can do that shit. I done sold 5 mill ta her one."

"Uh-huh. And we still waitin on that new album. You better get buzy, brotha. B.I.G. and 2Pac comin fuh yo' ass."

He grabbed my dick, makin me jump. "I'd rather *you* come fuh it." Yeah, he wants it *bad*: He been beggin me ta bang him. He been real crafty about it, too: When I was knocked out asleep after our marathon session, he covered my piece and tried slippin it inside of himself. (It almost worked, makin me wonder how many other niggaz he tried it wit'—and succeeded.) But I knew if I fucked him, there'd be no turnin back.

I pushed his hand off, lookin around. "Man, will you chill? You want somebody ta see?"

"Can't nobody see what's goin on under this table. But if you *really* wanna be discreet, we can make our exit and take this someplace else. Like my hotel room."

Is he fuh real?

"Nigga, I ain't *never* goin ta a hotel room wit' you again," I said, very matter-of-factly.

"Yo, you invited me up, remember? I ain't push my way in, and you ain't push me away."

"I ain't talkin about that, and you know it."

He pulled back. "Yo, man, you still ain't angry about what happened wit' Tha Camp, is you?"

"Yeah, mutha-fucka, I'm still angry about that shit."

He pleaded his case. "Yo, we was just havin some fun, brotha."

"Five niggaz jumpin on me, tryin ta get they jollies 'n' shit? That ain't fun," I barked.

99

"Yo, man, you might be angry about it now, and you mighta been angry at first when we su'prised yo' azz, but you got right inta tha swing of thangz. They had a good fuckin time samplin yo' azz. No, no, how you say it? Yeah...*jood*."

"Mutha-fucka, I don't know how you could even be smilin up in my face after some shit like that."

That smile turned inta a Cheshire grin."You enjoyed it."

"You set my ass up."

"Ha, you can say that again!" He laughed.

I turned away from him. "That shit ain't funny."

"Nigga, you know it was feelin jood ta ya. You was fightin wit' Tha Camp fuh like a few minutes, tryin ta pretend you wasn't likin it, like you ain't wanna do it, when you was and ya did."

Yeah, I liked it. After our sexcapade, I was too hot ta trot. He lit a fire under my azz and I was achin fuh some mo', but I wasn't plannin on satisfyin that hunger until I got back ta New York. Which is why that whole episode wrecked me. I really thought them niggaz was gonna rape me. Well, in a way they did. I didn't go ta that hotel room ta kick it wit' any of 'em. Shit, I ain't know anybody else was gonna be there. (Malice lied and said he needed ta get sumthin from one of his boyz visitin from outa town and we'd be headin back out.) And while I mighta got inta it after awhile (wit' all them fingers fondlin, hands rubbin, tongues trailin, lips kissin, and teeth bitin on ya, ain't no way you not gonna get turned on), how was I gonna fight off all them mutha-fuckaz?

We talkin 'bout some true gangstaz, G, straight-up hard-core niggaz: They ain't gotta strap cuz that killa look they wear 24-7 is they weapon, and they was all bumped up like they just got outa da pen and ain't been doin nuthin but pumpin up. It was truly a wild prison scene, and I was da new punk on da cell block.

I waved him off. "That shit was still foul, man. You was so wrong."

He sucked his teeth. "Nigga, you'd think we ran a train on yo' ass. Ha, if we wanted ta, we coulda, and ya know it. But we wasn't havin that kinda party. Them niggaz knew that if anybody was gonna get on up in *that azz* it was gonna be me. They knew you was off-limits when it came ta that."

"Oh, they did?"

"Yeah. All ev'rybody wanted was a little taste. It was yo' initiation."

I looked at him. "Say what?"

"We was breakin you in, man. Bringin you inta Tha Camp. And, if ya didn't know it already, you passed tha test. You got high marks, my man. Them niggaz want cha back fuh a encore 'n' shit. Once again, you lived up ta yo' initials, brotha: *RER*," he growled.

"Well, there ain't gonna be no repeat performance. You can quote me on *that*."

"Not even fuh me?"

"Hell, no."

"Oh, come on, why you wanna be like that? You know you liked that sample you got."

"Man, I done told you, I got somebody."

He eased back, frownin. "Ha, you wasn't throwin him up in my face when you was throwin yo' azz at my tongue."

I cut my eyes at him.

He looked around. "And, where *is* this nigga? How come he ain't here wit' you? He *stoo*pid ta let you go out by yo'-self. I'd never let a phyne nigga like you outa my sight."

"Don't worry about him, a'ight?"

"Man, when you gonna admit it?"

"Admit what?"

"That that *some*body you got ain't givin ya ev'rythang ya need."

"And *you* can?"

"Yo, don't knock me 'til ya done tried *all* of me, baybay."

"I ain't yo' baybay, a'ight?"

"You know you wanna be."

I laughed. "I do?"

"Yeah, you do. You say you don't, but yo' body keeps sendin out a diff'rent vibe, brotha. And if you was that mad at me and ain't want me up in yo' face, you woulda done told me ta step. But that's a'ight, cuz I got yo' number—and it's tha right one, baybay, *uh-huh*."

All I could do was shake my head. "Nigga, you just never quit."

"That's becuz I always get what I want. You gonna be *all* mine one day." He leaned in. "Haven't ya heard?" That's another track from his CD, where he borrows again from Patrice Rushen. She got some nice checks from his record label fuh them permissions. "I'm gonna get ya."

"Nigga, what you gonna get is lockjaw workin that trap like that all tha time," I smirked.

"But serious, brotha, ya need ta come by my room Wednesday nite. Some of tha East Coast members in Tha Camp wanna meet ya. They don't believe you on tha down low; they wanna see ya fuh themselves."

Now, it don't su'prise me that there's a lota brothas in hip-hop who are, as he put it, "on tha down low." Tha Camp is one of tha groups they got ta hook up and hang out. (I guess they got a North and a South chapter, too.) Malice took me ta a Camp jam, where there was a whole lota drinkin, bluntin, and fuckin goin on. They had go-go boyz doin lap dances and a "darkroom," where ya could get ya groove on *and* off. (Yeah, Malice tried his best ta get me up in there.) But I gotta admit, I *was* su'prised ta see a few faces I never expected, like b-ballers from the Lakers and the Suns, footballers from the 49ers and the Seahawks, a coupla singers Little Bit told me he suspected of bein gay, and one *very* big movie star.

So I was curious about who else had a membership, especially if they in my neck of da woodz (like that New York Jet that stepped ta me at All-American's Xmas bash last year). "Who?" I asked.

But I wasn't gettin that info outa him. "I ain't tellin ya. If ya wanna know, ya gotta come ta my room."

"*Fuck* that."

His eyes focused on my ass. "Ha, you won't let me." He frowned. "Man, ain't nobody gonna rape you...unless you want 'em to."

"That shit ain't funny."

"Yo, you don't trust me?"

"*Hell*-fuckin-no."

"A'ight, then, I'll tell you what: You can bring yo' somebody wit' cha—I don't care."

I knew he had ta be jokin. Even if I was ta bring Little Bit, I bet this nigga would live up ta his name and say sumthin that would bring what we did ta tha light. I wasn't about ta let that happen. I know Little Bit called me when we was gettin it on; Malice saw I was gonna answer it, but after it stopped ringin, he made sure it wasn't gonna ring no mo' when he knocked it off tha hook.

So, I knew he *did* care, but gave him tha benefit of tha doubt. "You lyin."

"Nah, I ain't. Bring him. But don't be su'prised if he ditch yo' ass and go off wit' somebody else in Tha Camp."

"Ha, I don't think so. My Baby, he ain't like that. I'm all he need."

"Ha, but he ain't all *you* need."

"Yeah, whatever."

"Uh-huh, yeah, I know you down fuh *what*-ever. Uh…" He looked around. "You wanna sneak off ta tha stairwell?"

"No."

"Tha bathroom?"

"*No.*"

"C'mon. I could go fuh a squeeze of that Charmin, get a few licks in… Yo, ain't that some shit about Eazy?"

This nigga is *too* much. Fuh tha first five minutes of our convo, all he can talk about is gettin some, and then he just comes outa nowhere wit' that. But I was glad he changed tha topic, cuz I was gettin turned on. "Yeah, it is."

"Yo, that nigga shoulda been mo' careful, ya know? I told ev'ry nigga in Tha Camp, 'That shit ain't nuthin ta fuck around wit', so don't be stoopid and fuck around.'"

"Word-'em-up, brotha."

"Yo, and ain't that some shit about him marryin befo' he died?"

"Yo, he did it ta protect his bank. He knew as soon as he went ev'rybody and they mama be makin a claim."

"True. But that's still gonna happen. Nigga had like six or seven kids by diff'rent females. Talk about bein fruitful and multiplyin. I understand why he did it. But marryin somebody, 'til death do you part, and you *know* you gonna be dyin? That shit is *wack*."

"Yeah."

"But if it wasn't fuh him, I wouldn't be here. So, I give props ta tha brotha, puttin West Coast niggaz on da map. May he rest in peace."

Just then, there was a whole lota commotion near tha entrance. We both stood up.

"Ah, I guess she here," I said.

"It's about time. Day-um. Yo, you wanna come over ta my table?"

"Nah. I better stay here, wait 'til Angel gets back."

"Y'all both can come. Shit, is he Puerto Rican? My boyee, Ace, he loves him some Puerto Rican Papis. We can all hook up fuh a foursome."

"I don't think so."

"A'ight, a'ight. But, yo, don't leave after tha show is over. My lady should be comin in any minute now. She gonna want yo' autograph."

Yeah, he married. And he got 6-year-old twins, too: A son and a daughter—Malice Jr. and Melanie. He say our both havin "juniors" who are tha same age ain't a coincidence, either.

"A'ight," I said.

He held out his hand. As we did tha brotha shake and hug, he squeezed my ass.

I pulled away. "Nigga, what tha fuck you think you doin?"

"I'm sayin good-bye. What tha fuck it feel like?" he snickered.

"Uh-huh. I'll check you later. *Much* later."

He winked. He bopped off.

Little Bit stood over me. "So, how you feel?"

Hmm…I'm coughin, I'm weezin, I'm snifflin, I'm sneezin. I guess I ain't feelin too jood, hunh?

I squinted. I shivered. "How I look?"

"You really wanna know?"

I shrugged.

"Bad."

I frowned. "Thanks a lot."

He handed me a tissue. "Here. Blow."

I sat up. I did. "Ah. I'm so congested."

"I know. I hear it. Let me take your temperature."

"Lit—"

He stuck a thermometer in my mouth. He put his hand ta his mouth. "How do you expect me to know how sick you are if you talk?"

I took it out. I grinned. "Ha, you can always stick it in…"

He slapped my hand. "You're a mess, even when you're sick. Now put that thermometer back in."

I did. He left tha room. A minute later he came back wit' a tray. He placed it on top of tha dresser. He took tha thermometer out of my mouth.

He studied it. "Hmm. Ninety-nine point one. Well, this is what you get, tryin to look cute, runnin around in that jacket last night."

"But it wasn't cold, Baby."

"You know better than that, Pooquie. Just because the temperature goes up 10 degrees doesn't mean you can start dressing like it's spring."

"But it *is* spring."

"Figuratively, maybe. But literally? I think not."

He sat tha tray down in fronta me. There was a steamin teapot, a coffee cup, Dayquil, TheraFlu, Vicks cough drops, and Tylenol.

"Day-am, Little Bit. You expect me ta take all of this?"

"No. Drink the tea first. It has whiskey in it."

"Whiskey? You tryin ta get me drunk and take advantage of me?"

"Uh, I wouldn't need whiskey to do that, now would I?" I blushed.

"After you drink it, go back to sleep. If the cold hasn't

been knocked out by the time I get back, we'll take it from there."

"When you get back?"

"Yes. Today's a half-day in school, but then I have that meeting with the lawyer. So I won't be back until 3."

I fuhgot that he and *Your World* finally agreed on tha terms fuh his settlement. They claim they ain't admittin they discriminated against him, but all tha funds they gonna be shellin out tell a diff'rent story. Shit, he prob'ly gonna be a millionaire befo' me. "But, Baby, can't cha do it another day?"

"No. I have to sign the agreement today, before they come up with something else to nitpick about. I want this over with and that first check in my hand before Easter."

"But what about me?"

"Pooquie, you'll be all right."

I hugged myself. "No I ain't, Baby. It feels like I'm gonna die."

He shook his head. "All you have is the beginnings of a bug."

"How you know?" I rubbed my chest. "It feels like pneumonia ta me."

"Have you ever *had* pneumonia?"

"No."

"Then how would you know what it feels like if you've never had it?"

"I know, a'ight."

"Well, *I* know, because my uncle and my grandmother had it. And, believe me, your temperature would be much higher, and you'd be so weak and in so much pain you wouldn't want to speak. We'd be rushing you to the hospital right now."

"But, Baby, I don't wanna be by myself."

He grasped my face. "It won't be for long, OK? You should be resting, not getting worked up. Now, put on those pajamas and make sure you bundle up when you go back to sleep."

He tweaked my nose. He got up. He was about ta leave when…

"*Yo!*"

He stopped. He turned. He smiled. "You bellowed?"

"You ain't gonna kiss me jood-bye?"

"No, I ain't gonna kiss you jood-bye."

"Why not?"

I sneezed.

He laughed. "That's why. If we're both sick, who's gonna take care of *us*?"

I wiped my nose. I pleaded my case. "Aw, c'mon, Little Bit. I need some TLC, too."

He shook his head. "You can be such a big baby." He came back. He pecked me on my forehead. "Happy now?"

"Nah. I mean, you coulda gave it ta me on my lips."

"You should be happy I didn't *blow* you a kiss!"

I frowned.

"But don't worry. When I get back, I'll rub you down." Now, ya know that frown turned upside down. "Yeah?"

"Yeah. From head to toe."

"Then whatcha standin there fuh? Leave so ya can hurry up this way again!"

"Uh-huh. Now you want me to go, hunh? I'll call you around noon." He nodded at tha tray. "The whole pot, OK?"

"A'ight."

"I'll be Black. Love you."

"Love you, too, Baby. Thanks."

"Anytime, Pooquie. Anytime."

"Pooquie! Pooquie! Wake up!"

I did. I was shakin and sweatin. "Huh?"

He was cradlin me. "You were having a nightmare."

"I—I was?"

"Yeah. It was just like Tuesday night. You were scream-ing, 'Why me, why me, why did it have to be me?' Do you remember what you were dreaming about?"

I did. I could still see it. I wish I couldn't, but I did. And there was no way I was gonna tell him about it. "Uh, nah, nah, Baby…I don't remember."

"Oh, no, that's terrible. That means you'll probably

keep dreaming it until you do."

"Huh?"

"I believe that's the way it is. I had this nightmare, and until I knew what it was about, until I could clearly see it while it was happening, I couldn't stop dreaming it."

"Yeah? Uh, you remember what you was dreamin about?"

He remembered; his face said it all. "About...about dying."

"About...dyin?"

He sighed. "Yeah."

"You mean, you was dyin in tha dream?"

He nodded yes.

"That's scary, Baby."

"Tell me about it. I was so freaked out by it that I didn't sleep for a week."

"A whole week?"

"Yeah. I just knew I would keep dreaming it, and I was scared it would come true. Some of my dreams before that had come true. And this one, like the others, was so real."

"You wanna tell me about it?"

He did. His head found its place on my chest, and I held him.

"I was in the hospital, hooked up to this machine. My mother, Anderson, Aunt Ruth, Uncle Tweedle, Alvin, Calvin...they were all standing over me, crying. And Adam...he was holding my hand. He kept telling me to fight, to fight it. And when I tried to say something to him…I was so frail and weak…my eyes closed. And the machine started to hum."

"It started ta hum?"

"Yeah, you know, an extended beeping sound. And on the machine's screen, there was a line running across the center."

"Ah. That's horrible, Little Bit."

"Mmm-hmm. It wasn't until I faced it that I realized why I was having it."

"And why was you?"

"Because I wasn't dealing with my Uncle Russ's death. I guess I kinda felt guilty that I was the last one to see him alive and I didn't see it. That I didn't know. That I shoulda been able to save him."

"But you know you couldn't, Baby."

"I know, but then I didn't. You usually have that kind of dream when something is really troubling you. Is anything wrong?"

"Nah."

"You sure? You know you can tell me."

"I know, Baby."

"Uh, you still can't remember what the dream was about?"

"Nah."

"Do you know how you felt during it?"

Uh-oh. "How I felt?"

"Yeah. Sometimes, even if you can't see it, you feel the emotions that gripped you."

I could remember that, too, but wasn't about ta give

that one up, either. "I don't know."

"Well, if you do remember anything, you know you can tell me. I'm here for you."

"I know, Baby. Thanks."

"Anytime, Pooquie. Anytime."

I squeezed him tighter; he returned my squeeze. We was quiet fuh a minute, our hearts beatin tagether.

"Well, you probably don't wanna go back to sleep just yet, hunh?" he asked.

"Ha, how you guess?"

"Well, how about some hot chocolate?"

"That sounds jood."

"OK."

We kissed.

He climbed outa bed. He turned and smiled. "I'm sure we can find another use for the whipped cream." He winked.

I giggled.

"Hi, Daddy…"

I came in his room. I sat down next ta him on his bed. He was dressed in his Elmo pajamas.

"So…what's up, my man?"

"Um…did Mommy tell you?"

"She couldn't tell me ev'rything. So, go 'head."

He folded his hands. He put 'em in his lap. He sighed. "Um…me and Corey and Chad and Jesse we were on line getting our lunch, and…" He was tryin ta get it all out too fast and wasn't catchin his breath.

I put my arm around him. "Take yo' time, man."

He breathed. "Uh…Corey, he asked if you and Mommy

117

married. And I said no. And then Corey said…he said…
he said that I come from a broken home."

"And what you say?"

"I said…I said, 'No, I don't'. And he said I did because
my mommy and my daddy, they not married. And if
they not married…that means I don't come from a real
family. I come from a broken home."

"Now, what I tell you 'bout list'nin ta what them
folks say?"

"I know, Daddy."

"If you know, then why you hit him?"

"Because, Daddy, he…he…" He started cryin.

I picked him up and put him on my knee. He snuggled up against me and I wiped his tears.

"C'mon, Li'l Brotha Man. Tell me."

He sniffled. "He was talking about you and Mommy,
Daddy. And he wouldn't stop saying it. It made me angry."

I cradled him. "I know, my man, I know. But people
always gonna say things about you, about me, about
Sunshine, that ain't gonna be nice. But you can't let 'em
get ta ya like that."

"I…I didn't know what to say, Daddy."

I shook him, grinning. "Ha, you might not have, but
yo' fists sho' did."

He shrugged.

"Man, he wanted ya ta hit him, so he could show you up.
They all was just waitin fuh you ta do sumthin like this."

"What do you mean, Daddy?"

"Remember how I told you that they wanna make

ev'rybody see that, cuz you Black, you ain't s'pose ta be there, and that they gonna do ev'rything they can ta prove it?"

He nodded yes.

"Well, it happened. He was wrong and he's tha one that should be suspended, but it's prob'ly gonna be you."

"I'm sorry, Daddy. I didn't do jood."

"Nah, you didn't do jood. But that's a'ight. I don't do jood all tha time. We only human. You was lookin out fuh me 'n' Sunshine. It musta hurt ta hear him say that, hunh?"

He nodded yes, again.

"Yeah, I think I know how you feel."

"You do?"

"Yeah. Nobody made me feel bad about it but… sometimes, I would just feel like…like I wasn't jood enuff cuz…cuz my Pops wasn't around. You lucky cuz you got both of us in yo' life."

"But why would he say that, Daddy? I never said anything mean about him."

"Sometimes people hafta be mean so they can feel better about themselves, feel better than you. You ain't broken, is you?"

"No."

"And me and yo' Moms ain't broken, is we?"

"No."

"So how you gonna come from a broken home? That don't make no sense. He prob'ly just jealous cuz you got both of us. His parents might be married, but that don't mean they happy. He prob'ly wish he had parents like you."

119

We was quiet fuh a bit. I rocked him in my arms.

"Daddy?"

"Yeah, my man?"

"How come you and Mommy not married?"

Uh-oh. I knew this was comin sooner or later, but I was truly hopin fuh later. *Much* later.

I sighed real heavy. "Li'l Brotha Man…see…we was really young when we had you. If I'm 22 now and you 6, how old was I when you was born?"

He did tha math, tappin his temple. "Sixteen, Daddy."

"Right. See, that's too young ta be havin a baby and it's too young ta be gettin married. But even tho' we ain't get married we wasn't gonna give you up ta nobody."

"You mean, give me up for adoption?"

He is just *too* sharp. "Yeah. Whatcha know about that?"

"That's when the baby is raised by somebody else and not the parents. My friend Chad is adopted."

"You got it. We was busy tryin ta raise you. We wasn't worried about bein husband and wife."

"Well, why didn't you and Mommy do it later on?"

Day-um. He knows how to ask them follow-up questions, don't he? "Cuz, Li'l Brotha Man, we…we…we just stopped bein in love."

"Why?"

"Uh…cuz…I don't know how ta explain it, man. Sometimes that happens. People…they change. Things change. People, they grow apart. They grow up. I know that's what happened ta me. Havin you forced me ta. But, we might not be in love wit' each other, but we do love and care for each other. It's just not tha kinda love that's s'pose ta be between a man and a woman that get married. You understand?"

"I think so."

I turned him ta face me. "But me 'n' Sunshine not bein in love ain't got nuthin ta do wit' you. We ain't never gonna stop lovin you. That ain't never gonna change. You know that, right?"

"Yes, I do."

"It don't matter what you say or what you do, even if you get in trouble at school. A'ight?"

"Uh-huh."

"Jood."

"Daddy?"

"Yeah?"

"Can I have a hug?"

"Man, you ain't even gotta ask. Anytime you want one, just take it, a'ight?" I smiled.

He smiled, too. "OK."

I gave him a big, long one. It seemed like he ain't wanna let go.

"Now, you gonna hafta go back ta school and fix this."

He frowned. "Do I have to?"

"Yeah, you hafta."

He ain't look too happy about that.

"And I know it's gonna be hard fuh ya ta do, but you gonna hafta say sorry ta that boy."

"But he should have to say sorry to *me*, Daddy," he argued, pointin ta himself.

121

"I know he should. And I'm gonna make sure he do."

His face lit up. "Oh, are you gonna come with me, Daddy?"

I squeezed him. "You know I am."

He grinned.

"But two wrongs don't make a right, do it?"

"No, it don't."

"So, you gotta face whatcha did. He mighta pushed you ta do it and he mighta deserved it, but you still broke a rule at school. If he was botherin you you shoulda told a teacher. But we'll see that dean. We'll get ev'rything straightened out. And ya know you gonna hafta be punished, right?"

His eyes bugged. "Punished?"

"Yeah."

He put his head down. He clasped his hands.

"I'm gonna talk ta Sunshine about it."

"OK," he whispered.

"But don't worry. We ain't gonna take away yo' allowance."

His head lifted. He had a big ol' Kraft grin on his face. I laughed. He did, too.

"So, you learn anything from this?"

"Uh-huh."

"What?"

"That, even if somebody says something bad about me, you, or Mommy, that doesn't mean I can hit them."

"Right. Just ignore them. And if they really start ta get ta you, tell somebody."

"OK. And Mommy says a friend doesn't call you names like that, so Corey isn't my friend."

"No, he ain't. If he apologizes and you wanna still be friends wit' him, that's yo' choice. But if not, fine. You can find other friends."

"Uh-huh. And Mommy said it's wrong to use violence to solve a problem."

I nodded in agreement. "Mommy is right."

"And I also learned that my teacher, Miss Greene, is wrong, Daddy."

"Whatcha mean?"

"She said, 'Sticks and stones will break your bones, but names will never hurt you.' But they do."

I sighed. "Yeah, my man. They do."

★ ★ ★

I read Li'l Brotha Man a story and put him ta bed. Then I went inta tha bathroom and cried my eyes out. It's times like these that make you wanna lock yo' kids up and never let 'em outa tha house. It hurt me so much ta know somebody would hurt him like that.

I found Sunshine dressed in a pink robe and slippers, sittin on tha sofa, watchin TV. I plopped down next ta her, puttin my head back, sighin.

She turned ta me. "Well?"

"He don't wanna go back."

"I know you told him he has to."

"I did. I also told him I'd go back ta school wit' him."

"Ah. I'm sure he likes that idea."

"Yeah."

Silence.

"I can't believe that little cracker said that about him!" I snarled.

She huffed. "Raheim, you can't go into that principal's office tomorrow morning and call that boy a little cracker."

"I know. I ain't. But he gonna hafta apologize ta Li'l Brotha Man, too. Why he hafta say some shit like that?"

"Kids can be cruel."

"Sunshine, ain't no kid come up wit' some shit like that. He musta learned it from his parents."

"Probably. So what did you tell him?"

"I told him that there ain't no way he can come from a broken home cuz he ain't broken. And mommy and daddy ain't either."

"And what about hitting him?"

"I told him he can't go 'round hittin folks just cuz they say things he don't like."

"Mmm-hmm. I hear it was one fierce left hook."

We smiled. We sat in silence, watchin Max and Kyle go at it again on *Living Single*.

"He wanted ta know why we ain't married," I mumbled.

She turned ta me, her eyes wide. "He did?"

"Yeah."

"And what did you tell him?"

"That...that we was too young ta marry when he was born. And that...when people grow up, they sometimes grow apart…they fall outa love."

"Yeah. Some of us do."

Uh-huh, she was talkin about me.

"So, how do you think he should be punished?" she asked.

"I don't know. Whatever you think is a'ight wit' me."

"Uh-huh. Just pass the buck and make *me* the bad guy, right?"

"Nah, nah…whatever you think."

"Well, he just knows that we're going to take away his allowance, and something like this does warrant it. But," she grinned, "he *was* sticking up for himself *and* his parents."

I grinned, too. "Ha, yeah."

"Let's say…no TV except *Sesame Street* and *Reading Rainbow*, and he can't go outside for…two weeks. And he's been so happy about getting that allowance he's stopped asking about going to see the Ice Capades. If he does again, he can't go."

"That sounds jood ta me."

Silence.

"We never shoulda sent him there," I groaned.

She sucked her teeth. "Raheim, please, let's not start that again."

"Well, look at what happened. Ain't no way you gonna tell me some shit like that woulda happened at Carver or MLK."

"Yes, the same thing could have happened to him at Carver or King Elementary."

"Oh, come on, Sunshine! Ain't no white kids at Carver or MLK."

"Kids are kids, Raheim. Do you think Junior would have hurt less if those words came out of the mouth of another Black child?"

"Nah, nah, it's diff'rent, Sunshine, and you know it. It's that uppity attitude of them white folks at that school, thinkin they better than ev'rybody else."

"It's not the white folks at the school that hurt him. It's one child."

I waved off her comment, turnin away.

She grabbed my right hand wit' her left. "He'll be OK. He's strong. Just like his daddy."

I shrugged.

"**T**wenty five thousand *three hundred sixty four dollars?*"

I just stared at them digits: Two, five, comma, three, six, four. Five figures.

Well, this was da ultimate proof that, if I ain't made it yet, I was on my way. I knew that tally was gonna be up there, but *day-um*! One year I'm makin this much and tha next I'm payin it out?

"Little Bit, you sure this right?"

"Pooquie, that number is right. I've followed everything to the letter. Itemized deductions, write-offs, your dependents..."

Yeah, ain't this sumthin: I ain't my Mom's dependent no mo', she's mine. But even that ain't seem ta bring that tally down. "It just can't be right, Baby. That's too fuckin much."

"Well, when you think about it, it really isn't. The average American pays out about 10% of his or her income to the federal government in taxes each year. So that amount is about right."

"It might be about right, but that don't mean it is. I mean, writin a check fuh that much money?"

"You're playin in the big leagues now, Pooquie. The more you make, the more they take."

"Ha, not if you white."

"Hmm, just be glad that invisible Black tax didn't make that total higher."

I just stared at that total. "It's just *too* fuckin much, Baby."

He rubbed my head. "I know. But I'll tell you one thing: It's better to pay too much than pay too little."

"Ha, fuck that. I ain't givin them mutha-fuckas a penny extra."

"Mmm, them pennies add up. They find out you paid even a penny less than you did, and they'll accuse you of cheating them, start tacking on that interest and those penalties, and before you know it, you end up paying much, much more in the end."

I sat back. I huffed. "This just a fuckin crime. What tha fuck they gonna do wit' all this money?"

Little Bit smiled. "Ha, what else? Waste it."

"I can do so fuckin much wit' them funds. That's Jeep money 'n' shit."

"Mmm-hmm."

"Them funds could go ta payin fuh Mom's co-op. Shit, I could put a down payment on a house."

"Uh-huh."

"I could buy some more stocks or bonds, open up another CD. Or I could just drop it in Li'l Brotha Man's account. *Day-um.*"

"Yeah. I know."

I really wanted ta rip it up, but I tossed that tax form on tha table instead. "This shit is depressin."

"Uh-huh. It is. But look on the bright side."

I looked at him like he was trippin. "Tha bright side?"

"At least you've got the money to pay."

"*That's* s'pose ta be a bright side?"

"Yeah. You've heard all them stories about people havin their bank accounts frozen, their wages garnished, and losing their home, car, all their possessions. I think they auctioned off all of Willie Nelson's and Redd Foxx's stuff. They can be ruthless."

I frowned.

"What a way to spend a Friday night, hunh?" he asked.

I sighed. "Yeah."

He got *that* look in his eye. "We *could* be doin other things."

"We could, hunh?"

"Mmm-hmm. You should be payin *me* some taxes. You been holdin back on me."

Uh-oh. "Holdin back on you?"

He got up. He stood behind me, massagin my shoulders. "Yes. Your payment is late—and your account continues to accrue interest as we speak."

I grinned. "Oh, yeah?"

"Yeah. And besides, you also have to pay me for my tax services. So I think I'll have to collect two scoops." He slid his hands under my seat and squeezed my cheeks.

I chuckled. "Yo, I thought I got until April 15th ta pay up?"

"The government can wait, Pooquie. I can't." He started makin circles on top of my head wit' his tongue—sumthin he knew got my nipples hard and booty tinglin. And it was workin. But I wasn't about ta give in this time...

When he sat on my lap and proceeded ta tongue me down, I stopped him. "Hold up, Little Bit."

"What, Pooquie?"

"I...I don't feel like it."

"You...don't feel like it?" he repeated as if he heard me wrong.

"Nah."

Yeah, he knew he was hearin thangz. "*You* don't feel like gettin buzy?"

I nodded no.

He sighed heavily. "OK, Pooquie. What's wrong?"

"Whatcha mean?"

"Something is wrong when you don't wanna get buzy two weeks in a row. Hell, you're the one who usually has to remind me."

"I...I don't know, Baby. There's just a whole lot goin on, and...wit' this stuff happenin ta Li'l Brotha Man..."

"Mmm…you still worried about him?"

"Yeah." And I was, too. Li'l Brotha Man apologized ta Corey, and Corey apologized ta him. Corey's Pops was real understandin about tha whole thang. He told that dean that he didn't think Li'l Brotha Man should be suspended, and she agreed. But I know if he had come up there demandin that Li'l Brotha Man be kicked out, she woulda gladly gave Li'l Brotha Man his walkin papers. And I also knew that, no matter how sincere Corey mighta seemed, no matter how much Corey's Pops felt partly at fault since his boy was only repeatin things he heard his Pops say, and no matter how nice a face they all was puttin on it, Li'l Brotha Man was gonna still have a tuff time. He gonna be known as that Black kid who is violent and got a temper. Well, they prob'ly already thought he was violent and had a temper, but now they got proof. Folks might not go outa their way ta make things hard fuh him, but they ain't gonna make things easy.

Little Bit consoled me. "You know you don't have to, Pooquie. He'll pull through this. *We'll* pull through this."

He caressed my head. He smiled. I did, too.

"Uh, you sure I can't persuade you to let me have just a *little* taste?" he whispered.

"A little? How'm I gonna do that? I ain't got a little, I got a lot!"

We both laughed.

"Uh-huh, you sure do," he agreed. "But I'm talkin about you lettin me have a little taste of your big salad bowl."

"Uh…" Now, he knew how much I *loved* that. But ain't no way I could let him lick me wit'out stickin me. And he knew *that*, too. This was his way of gettin some. But I wasn't fallin fuh it. "Nah."

"No?"

"Nah."

"You don't want that booty basted and tasted? Hmph, now I *know* something is wrong."

"No, it ain't. You know if sumthin was wrong I would tell you. I'm justa little on edge right now."

He studied me. "Mmm…OK. But you better get *off* that edge soon, get them kinks out. Like T-Boz says, 'I like 'em attentive.'"

"Ha, don't I know it." I kissed him. "Ya know what I could go fuh right about now?"

"What?"

"A long hot bath wit' u. And I think it's my turn ta give *you* a rubdown." I blew in his right ear.

He giggled. He grinned. "Mmm. Your wishes are my command."

Sunshine wanted me ta stop by befo' I picked Li'l Brotha Man up from my Mom's. We sat at her dinin room table.

She took a deep breath. "I wanted to talk to you about something."

"I know. That's why I'm here, right? So, what else he do wrong?"

"I take it that the *he* you are referring to is Junior?"

"Yeah. Who else?"

"Well, this is not about Junior."

"It ain't?"

"No."

"Then who?"

"Me."

"You?"

"Yes, me."

"You wanna talk ta *me*…about *you*?"

"Yes. Are you surprised?"

"Uh, yeah. I mean, it's been a long time since…you know."

"Yes, I know. And that's what this is about."

"A'ight. I'm list'nin."

"Um…I've been dating a gentleman…for the past year. His name is Winston, and…we're getting serious."

"Why you tellin me?"

"Because I will be introducing him to Junior Easter weekend, and I wanted to tell you about Winston before he did. I didn't want it to be a surprise."

"Wait, hold up. You been seein somebody fuh a year, and Li'l Brotha Man ain't never met him, and you thinkin 'bout marryin him?"

"I didn't say I was thinking about marrying him."

"What else do 'getting serious' mean?"

"Ah…jood point. We haven't actually discussed marriage, but…I have a feeling it may be around the corner."

"Ain't that a long time ta be seein somebody, but they ain't meet yo' son?"

"Excuse me if I felt it was necessary for me to know this man before I did that."

"A'ight, a'ight, I ain't comin down on ya. So…he treat you jood?"

"Yes, he does. *Very* jood."

"Uh…you love him?"

"Yes, I do."

"And, if he pop *that* question…you gonna say yeah?"

"If he asked me, I do believe I would."

"Well…congratulations."

"What are you congratulating me for? I haven't said yes, and he hasn't even officially asked me."

"If y'all serious, he will. And when he do, you gonna say yeah, so it sounds like it's all set ta me. Uh, I just got one question."

"Uh-huh. And I know what it is."

"You do?"

"Yes, I do."

"Well, since you know, you tell me what it is."

"You want to know what type of relationship he and Junior will have, right?"

"No."

"No?"

"That's right, no."

"Then what is it?"

"Do he know L'il Brotha Man already got a Daddy?"

"Didn't I just say that but in a different way?"

"Ain't sound that way ta me."

"Yes, he already knows about you."

"He might know about me, but he don't know me."

"He won't have a problem with you so long as you don't have a problem with him."

"Meanin?"

"Meaning, he doesn't want to be your enemy so don't make him one."

"A'ight, a'ight. Just as long as he know his place."

"He will respect your place; just allow *him* a place in Junior's life also. He's not going to replace you. He's not taking over your role."

"Ha, he couldn't take over nuthin, any-ol'-way. Me 'n' Li'l Brotha Man, we two of a kind. Can't nobody replace me."

"I know. And it's because of that that I want you to work with Winston."

"Hunh?"

"Work with him."

"Whatcha mean, 'work with him?'"

"I don't want Junior to see or sense any tension or friction between you two. He should feel there is nothing wrong with his mommy being with a man who is not his father and that it's OK for him to like this man. You know how much he loves to see us together. And after that incident about coming from a broken home…if he sees that you and Winston get along, it won't be so hard for him to accept Winston."

"Yo, Li'l Brotha Man got enuff ta deal wit' at that school. I ain't gonna be givin him no grief cuz of this. Any-ol'-way, he prob'ly gonna love havin a stepdaddy. That means he can get two allowances." Hmm…he already got one in Little Bit, but she don't know it.

She laughed. "You better watch out, cuz he might like this stepparent thing so much, he'll be askin *you* about a stepmom."

"Yeah, well…"

Silence.

"Uh, I got one mo' question."

"OK…?"

"Uh…can I give you away?"

She was shocked ta hear that. "What?"

"Can I give you away…?"

"You…you *really* want to do that?"

"Yeah. You su'prised?"

"Well, yes, I am!"

"Why? You think I'm gonna be like, 'Yo, if I can't have ya, nobody can'?"

"No, but…this is definitely the other end of that spectrum."

"Yeah, well."

She grinned. "Hmm…sure you wouldn't want to *pay* for the wedding, too?"

"Now, let's not get cray-zee, a'ight?"

"Thank you, Raheim. I really appreciate that. If things come to pass…I think I would like that."

"Cool."

"Uh, there is one thing I would ask, and it may be hard for you to do."

"What?"

She hesitated. "Could you stop calling me Sunshine?"

I ain't expect ta hear that—and ya know I ain't like it. "*Why?*"

"Come on, Raheim, you know why. How would you like it if you got involved with a woman and her ex-boyfriend, the father of her child, continued to call her Sunshine?"

I shrugged. "It's just a nickname."

"No, it's not. It's a very special nickname from a very special time. It may make Winston uncomfortable."

"A'ight, a'ight. But I don't know what I'm gonna call you."

"How about the name my mother gave me?"

"But...*Crystal*...it's so...so plain and—"

"Ordinary, yes, I remember. But please, try to work on it. At least when he's around. OK?"

"A'ight. *Day-um*, this brotha must be sumthin special ta be puttin me thru these kinda changes."

"How do you know he's a brother?"

I jumped back in my seat, almost falling out of it. "*Say what?*"

She pointed ta me. "April fool!" She laughed.

I wasn't laughin. "Uh-huh."

"Yes, he is a special man."

"He *gots*ta be, cuz you got jood taste," I boasted.

She grinned. She nodded. "Yes, I do."

I t's hard tryin ta find sumthin ta talk about wit' someone ya don't wanna talk ta.

Well…it's not that I *don't* wanna talk ta tha Old Man (that's what I call him). If that was tha case, I wouldn't even be meetin him once a month fuh lunch or dinner. It's just that…well…after so many years of *not* havin him around, I don't know what ta say ta him. Yeah, I'm still dealin wit' and workin on my anger toward him. Even he knows that it ain't gonna go away overnite. But while I wanna get ta know him, I also wanna make sure he knows he gotta prove himself. I ain't makin it easy fuh him; shit, why should I? He sho' ain't make it easy fuh us. I guess I wanna make him suffer some, give him a little taste of what he gave us.

So when we hook up, he's doin most of tha talkin. He comes up wit' tha topic and when we seem ta have finished wit' it, he changes it. Tha only thang I usually pick is tha place we'll meet. This time it's Dojo's, a Japanese-American spot in tha East Village; ta my su'prise, they got some of tha best fried chicken I ever tasted. Most of tha time he wants ta talk about me, Li'l Brotha Man, or my Moms. So I was su'prised when he came outa nowhere wit'...

"Whatcha think about this O.J. situation?"

We had never discussed anything in tha news befo'. And of *all* tha things he coulda picked in tha news ta talk about...

"Ain't nuthin ta think about," I grumbled.

"Whatcha mean?"

"It ain't nuthin ta think about, and *he* ain't nuthin ta think about."

"Now, don't be comin down on brother O.J."

I cut my eyes. "He ain't no brotha."

"He sure do look like it to me."

"He ain't been actin like it tha past 20 years."

"Oh, just because the man don't live in South Central and he plays golf, that mean he ain't a brother?"

I had promised myself that this was one conversation I wasn't gonna have wit' anybody, but sumthin made me go there, anyway. "Nah. He ain't a brotha cuz he sacrificed himself—and us. He coulda lived in Brentwood and teed off all he wanted. But he just didn't want tha jood life, he wanted tha *white* life. And now his ass is payin fuh it."

" 'He wanted the white life, and now he's payin for it?' " he repeated, as if he didn't believe what I just said.

"Yeah. He got himself da ultimate prize—a white woman. And when she didn't want him no mo', he killed her."

"How you know? Were you there?" He was a little testy.

I threw it right back at him. "No, I wasn't, but his blood was."

"Yeah, that's what they say."

"So, what, you think they planted it?"

"It wouldn't be the first time."

Hmm…that was an openin. I guess I should bite, right? "Uh…Moms said…she said they tried framin you."

"Did she tell you the whole story?"

"Nah."

Silence.

I guess he wanted me ta ask him ta tell me. So I did. "Uh…what happened?"

He put tha tip of his left thumb in his mouth. Where have I seen *that* befo'? Then he settled back in his chair. "Well, there used to be this liquor store on 127th and Madison. It was owned by this old Jewish man. He was held up by two men. They shot him three times—once in the head—and he was in a coma. The cash he had on hand and his wallet were stolen. As you can imagine, there was a lot of pressure on the police to find whoever did it."

Ain't that always tha case?

"Two days after it happened, I was driving… I don't remember where I was coming from now, but I do know I was going home. No sooner had I parked my car a block from our house had a whole swarm of cops surrounded me. I was thrown against my car, handcuffed, and hit in the head with a baton by one of those bastards, who was saying things like, 'You better be glad I didn't shoot *you* in the head, *nigger!*'"

He was shakin; he took a deep breath. Retellin it must be like relivin it.

"Of course, I was…there ain't a word to describe what I felt, how I felt, what I was going through. I know I didn't rob or kill anyone. But they said they found evidence that I did in my car, his bloodstained wallet. That made no sense. I mean, even if I had done it, why would I keep the man's bloodstained wallet in my car?

"Turns out, it was left at the crime scene and they planted it there to scare me into confessin or rattin out somebody else. Maybe they were hopin I heard through the grapevine who did it. They knew they couldn't go to no D.A. with just a bloodstained wallet. But nothin gets in the way of New York's Finest doin their job. Not even the truth."

Ain't *that* tha truth?

"They weren't going to let me go; they wanted the city to think they had the person who did it, even though they knew they didn't. And because I already had a record, they could justify my being held and questioned."

I didn't know if it was sumthin I should ask, but I did

anyway. "Uh, what was you arrested fuh befo' that?"

He considered it. I guess he really didn't wanna tell me. "I…I got into a fight at a bar and…was arrested for assault. Public drunkenness. Disorderly conduct. I spent four days in jail. I pled guilty and got a suspended sentence. I vowed after that that I would never get drunk again and put your mother through that."

"I guess you ain't keep that promise."

"Back then, no. But I've been clean for eight years."

Hmm… "Is that why you only drink water?"

He was amused. "Ah, you noticed." He leaned forward and picked up his glass. "Yes. It's the one liquid that doesn't resemble anything I used to guzzle down. I may be clean, but I ain't cured." He put it back down. "So where was I?"

"Uh, they was holdin yo' record over yo' head…"

"Right. It's a leap to go from that to robbery and attempted murder. But, hey, ya can never put anything past them niggers, can ya?"

Uh-huh.

"Well, the only thing that saved me was a white man who didn't know me. If I hadn't been in his office the very moment that robbery happened…. He wouldn't give me a job, but he helped me get out of jail. And then he *still* wouldn't give me a job." He laughed. "It's a good thing I didn't throw away his number. I had your mom find it and call him. She came down to the station with him. He even had a copy of the application I filled out while I was there and an appointment book where he had my name as his interviewee. They couldn't argue with any of that.

"So, yeah, I do know what it's like to be one of the unlucky ones, chosen to take the fall for what someone else has done. I know too many of us who are sittin in prison right now because they were set up, tricked into confessin, or refused to point the finger at someone else."

I was feelin him and his story. I searched fuh sumthin ta say. "I…I'm sorry you had ta go thru that."

He nodded. "I'm sorry that I let it affect me the way it did. Something like that…it's gonna affect you. It's *still* affectin me today. Will be with me always. But I never shoulda allowed it to consume me. If I hadn't"—he looked at me—"things would've been different."

I looked down at my food. "Did you sue?"

"Sue who?"

I looked up. "Them cops. Tha city."

"Well, this was before we knew we could do that. We didn't have a Civilian Complaint Review Board back then. *Or* an Al Sharpton." He cleared his throat. "So…it's possible he *did* do it. I guess you could say that I saw him as a role model back in the day, so I just can't see him doin somethin like that. But it's also possible that, because of who he is, they knew that the way to make sure they could get him was to put that blood and that glove there to help their case."

Now why he wanna go back ta that juice-less mutha-fucka? "But if they wanted him they coulda got him a long time ago. I mean, these tha same cops who came ta his house mo' than once because he was beatin her. That's why white folks in shock. They thought he was one of *them.* Now that tha whole white world knows he was beatin his wife, he lookin mo' 'n' mo' like one of *us* ev'ry day."

"But you know we don't get the benefit of the doubt, no matter who we become, no matter how much money we make, no matter how much they say they accept us. And if he don't get it from us, who he gonna get it from?"

"Well, he ain't gettin it from me. He been livin da life of Smiley, chee-cheein it up wit' them white folks, and now all of a sudden he wanna cry Black on us like Clarence Thomas?"

"Hmm...sounds to me like you been doin a whole lota thinkin about this situation."

I shrugged.

"Everybody got a right to come back home, son."

I ain't really mind him callin me that. I mean, that's what I am, right? "Ya can't come back home if you ain't never really lived there."

Even *he* knew I wasn't talkin about O.J., but tried ta play it off. "True, true. But they tryin to crucify him. We just can't sit back and let 'em do it, no matter what he's done or *hasn't* done. It's happenin to Iron Mike. If folks wanna give him a parade, so what? It'll probably be the same for that rapper, what's his name? Uh, two packs of sugar?"

I couldn't help but laugh. "2Pac. Tupac Shakur."

His face lit up just like Li'l Brotha Man's when he gets

sumthin he likes. This was tha first time I had ever laughed in front of him. And, even tho' I was laughin at him, he ain't care. He grinned. "I was close."

I shook my head. "Not close enuff."

"Anyway, when he gets outa jail, he will have done his time. He shouldn't have to keep livin in a prison when he gets out. He shouldn't be punished again."

"I see whatcha sayin. But some of us deserve that second chance ta come back home. Some don't."

He nodded in agreement. We finished our food in silence.

He broke it as they took away our dishes. "Speakin of homes: I hear you're about to buy one for your mom."

"Yeah. We'll be signin tha papers next Saturday."

"I'm glad you were able to do that for her."

"Well, one of us had ta."

He frowned. He leaned in. He sighed. "I deserved that. And probably the digs before it. But I don't deserve to get them all the time, ya know?"

I shrugged a nod.

"I'd love to help you move her in…"

I wasn't too keen about hirin no movers. If anything came up missin or damaged, you'd hafta go thru a whole lota shit ta get them ta pay. Besides, I didn't want no strangers handlin this. I wanted ta see her out of tha old and inta tha new. She wasn't gonna be movin until tha end of May (givin her time ta pack what she want and throw away what she don't). So his strength would come in handy. I knew she'd like seein us collaboratin on sumthin; it'd be a jood late Mother's Day present.

I shrugged. "A'ight."

He was happy wit' that response—he was showin both rows of teeth. I guess he decided, since I was in a semi-jood mood, ta just go fuh broke. "Since you're in the making-dreams-come-true business, I was wondering if you could help one of mine happen."

I couldn't wait ta hear what it was. "I'm list'nin."

"I was hoping you'd agree to finally let me meet Li'l Brotha Man. It might be a little bit early to be thinking about this, but I'd love to have a birthday gathering for you two."

While he's been patient, Li'l Brotha Man been droppin bombs, not hints, about tha Old Man; he be askin about him wit'out really askin about him. Like last week he wanted ta know if there was such a thing as Grandparents Day, and some time befo' that he pointed out his friend's grandfather who picks her up ev'ry day after school. I know he's anxious and he's gonna love knowin tha Old Man; I just wanna feel jood about them meetin and know it's tha right time. Yeah, it's been almost a year since he came back but...I don't know. I guess I didn't feel that secure about it yet.

"Well," I began, "I think Sunshine may have sumthin planned."

"Crystal can come, too," he offered. "And, if they'd like, your mom, Crystal's mother, and...your friend, Mitchell, can also."

My friend?

147

Now, that *really* thru me fuh a loop. I know I only talk about Little Bit as Li'l Brotha Man's godfather. I ain't *never* called him my friend, not even *a* friend. And while he ain't say it *that* way, I knew what he meant (that pause befo' he said it said it all).

I truly was *not* goin there wit' him. "Uh, I'll ask and see."

"Jood." He smiled. I showed a little teeth on that one, too.

When our check came, he picked it up like he usually did. "Well, you ready?"

"Yeah." I went inta my pocket. "But I got this one."

He looked like he was gonna faint. "*You've* got it?"

I had never paid fuh one of our dates befo'. Ha, I had never *offered* ta pay. But sumthin told me...well...it was about time I did. I took tha check from him. "Yeah. No prob."

He was beamin from ear ta ear. "Well, thanks, son."

I gave him half a smile. "You welcome." I put a Lincoln on tha table fuh tha waitress.

We got up and headed fuh tha entrance. He put his hand on my shoulder. "Don't look now, but I believe your public is approaching."

She had been starin at me all thru lunch, whisperin and conf'rencin wit' a brotha she was sittin wit'. She had a magazine in one hand and a camera in tha other. That's what she musta left tha restaurant ta get.

"Um, excuse me. I didn't want to disturb you while you were eating."

At least she got some manners.

"Aren't you Raheim, the model?" Now *that* was

refreshin— she knew my name. Most folk who recognize me usually ask "Aren't you that guy in the All-American ad?" She pointed ta my pic in *The Source*. I was wearin some A-A boxers.

I smiled. "That's me."

"Oh, could I *please* have your autograph?"

I took it. "Who do I make this out ta?"

"Charlie."

"Charlie?" I questioned.

"Yes."

Uh-huh…"Charlie," as in tha brotha seated at tha table wit' her. He was tryin ta be cool about it, watchin me sign. Tha Old Man caught it, too.

As I wrote, she checked us both out. "My, you two could almost be twins. Are you his brother?"

He grinned. "No, I'm not. But God bless you for that!"

He looked over at me. I guess he was givin me tha op of sayin who he was or not. I motioned toward him wit' my head. "He ain't my brother. He's my Pops." I had never called him that ta his face befo'.

And, becuz I didn't, *his* face was a neon-sign.

She was su'prised. "*You* are his *father*? You look so *young*."

He continued ta glow. "I *am* young."

She giggled. "Oh, could I take a picture with you both? It'll be clear where you got your good looks from. Like father, like son."

He smiled. "Well, thank you for that. But I'd prefer not to be in the spotlight with my son. I *will* take a picture of you two, if you'd like."

"Oh, please." She handed him her camera.

He took it.

"And can I get one of you by yourself?" she asked.

"Of course," I said.

She took it.

"Thank you so much. And good luck in your career."

"Thanks."

She nodded at tha Old Man, took her magazine, and headed back ta her table.

We turned ta tha cashier, and I was about ta give her two Jacksons when he beat me ta tha punch.

"I was gonna pay," I protested.

"I know. But it's not every day I get mistaken for being in my 20s by a beautiful woman—*or* get called Pops by my son." He winked. "This one is on *me*."

I shoved tha bills back in my pocket. "Thanks."

"You can pick up our next tab, next month."

I nodded. "A'ight."

APRIL 3rd, 10:30 a.m.

Located just up tha block from the Apollo on 125th Street, Hookin Up Headz is one of tha few barbershops I know of that is open on Monday. Black, who's been runnin tha place wit' his Pops fuh seven years, ain't stoopid—he knows brothas need a quick touch-up after tha weekend befo' they head back ta tha plantation. So, he starts snippin, shavin, 'n' shapin 'em up at 6 A.M.—and tha place be packed. Angel's 'do needed some stylin so we fell up in there *after* tha early mornin rush.

You can always count on some deep dialogue goin down in tha shop, and Black (who is so light-skinned ya gotta look twice ta make sure he is one of da Tribe; that big, wide nose is tha true marker) is always at tha center of tha convo. When we walked in, he was pontificatin about, as he called it, "tha mistrial of tha century." ("These crackers know damn well that if he had killed his first wife, they wouldn't give a shit about this case.") When Angel hopped in his chair, he started goin down tha cast of characters: givin Johnnie Cochran his props ("That's one smart-azz nigga…got all them crackers runnin scared") but doggin out Judge Ito ("Johnnie just walkin all over his ass"), Chris Darden ("He dumber than he look if he think he on that team cuz they *really* believe he was tha best man fuh tha job"), Marcia Clark ("That bitch need some *dick*… I bet she hate men"), even Denise Brown ("She and her family wasn't complainin about O.J. whippin Nicole's ass when he was writin them those checks") and Fred Goldman ("That mutha-fucka act like his son was tha first person ever murdered").

But you know who got tha worst of it.

"I am so *fuckin* tired of folks makin a fuss over that punk," Black almost shouted. "Niggaz act like he Malcolm or Martin and shit, about ta be assassinated."

I could agree wit' that. "Yo, I hear ya, brotha. What that mutha-fucka ever done fuh us?"

"Ha, not a *God*-day-um thang. He gettin just what he deserve, leavin his queen fuh that white girl. But all my Pops can say is, 'We gotta be there for him 'cause he one of us.'"

"Yeah. My Pops feel tha same way."

WHOA! Did I just say that? It was…well, it felt… kinda right. Kinda…good. Not *jood*, just good. I gotta get useta it.

"Oh, yeah? Don't tell me he yo' Pop's hero, too…?" I nodded. "Sumthin like that."

"Whatever. Mo' like a *ze*-ro. I don't care how well that punk ran wit' a football. Fuhget that sellout. Let's talk about a real Black man. Ain't that some shit about Eazy?"

"Yeah," me 'n' Angel both sighed.

"Man, it's almost enuff ta scare ya inta bein celibate," Black argued.

Angel smiled. "Yeah, but we know it ain't, right?"

Black laughed. "Man, you know it! Ain't no way I'm givin up pussy. When I get tha urge, I *gots*ta merge."

Me 'n' Angel looked at each other and gave him that hi-five nod (twistin both of our heads back and slowly snappin 'em forward). This was one of them moments when ya gotta play it cool but not too cool. Black is a hard-core hetero, and if he got wind that he had anybody in his shop that did, as he once put it, "tha bugaboo" (fuckin another brotha in tha azz), he'd freak—especially if they looked like, dressed like, walked like, and talked like him. *That* would rock his world.

"But it's fucked up," he continued. "They done found another way ta kill us."

Angel's eyebrows raised. We had been down this road befo' wit' him; Angel decided ta take that trip again. "C'mon, Black. You mean you think *this* a conspiracy against tha Black man, too?"

Black glared at him in disbelief. "Mutha-fucka, tha reason tha Black man is here *is* a conspiracy." He looked at me, pointin ta Angel. "Where you *find* this nigga?"

I chuckled.

"Man, why you think so many of us dyin from it?" he explained, puttin tha finishin touches on Angel's cut. "They scarin us inta gettin a test done, and tha next thang ya know, they hookin you up wit' HIV."

Hmm…now that's sumthin I ain't need ta hear right now. But I had ta know how he came ta this conclusion. "Man, you sayin they makin people sick on purpose?"

"*Hell,* yeah," he answered, like it was obvious.

Angel wasn't buyin it. "Man, that's cray-zee."

"Oh, yeah? Tell that ta tha folks I know it done happened ta."

"Man, you lyin!" Angel accused.

"Nah, I ain't. They tell you ta get a regular check-up, you know, *preventive* medicine. You all healthy and shit, and then months later, you dyin. I'm tellin you, that's why so many of us don't go ta no doctor. We know better. Remember Tuskegee, man. Never fuhgive, never fuhget."

"You really think they plottin on us like that?" I asked.

He gave *me* one of them "Nigga, *pleeze*" looks. "Man, ev'rythang's a part of tha plot. It ain't no coincidence that there's more of us in jail than college. They lockin niggaz up fuh five years fuh havin a vial of crack on 'em. Under that 'quality of life' bullshit, Fooliani is havin niggers arrested fuh just *standin* while Black. And Pataki wanna bring back tha *death penalty*?" He shook his head. "We ain't got tha capital, so you *know* we gonna get tha pun-ishment." He held up a mirror fuh Angel.

Angel checked himself out. "Yo, I heard they done brought back tha chain gang in Arizona." He approved of the back.

Black switched tha mirror ta tha front. "Ha, there's a picture fuh ya. Bruthaz wit' chains around they ankles. It's bad enuff so many of us walkin around wit' 'em on our brains."

When he OK'd tha front, Angel looked at me. We was thinkin tha same thang: He talkin about himself.

Angel decided ta take over tha Q 'n' A. "So what, Black, you think AIDS is sumthin they made up?"

He unfastened and took off Angel's neck wrap. "*Hell–fuckin-yeah.* A disease just don't pop up outa nowhere. And they comin up wit' sumthin new ev'ry day. They still tryin ta explain how Magic got it but not his wife and kids."

"Like wit' Eazy, they say you can have it and not pass it on," I added.

Black frowned. "Man, if that's tha case, then it don't matter if you use a condom. Nuthin but propaganda, them tryin ta keep our numbers down. *Fuck* that."

"So...you don't wear condoms?" I said, more ta myself, as Angel rose outa tha chair. Black got like five kids by three diff'rent sistas (maybe he tryin ta keep up wit' Eazy) so I kinda already knew tha answer ta that question.

"Nah. If it's somebody I really know, I don't. They just

be gettin in tha way, spoilin tha mood. Yo, I can't be puttin him in park when he ready ta ride, ya know what I'm sayin?"

Angel jumped in. "Man, you better buckle up. Ain't no cure." He handed Black his green.

"Man, you think they gonna create sumthin they can't contain? AIDS is a industry. They makin too much money off it ta break out that vaccine. And cuz we ain't useta takin all them toxins they say will make you better, we dyin quicker. That's what really killed Eazy."

Angel chuckled. "Man, you become a Muslim and shit?"

"You ain't gotta be no Muslim ta know what time it is. All you gotta do is open yo' eyes—and recognize. Yo, like PE say, 'Don't believe the hype.'"

"Well…" I started, gettin up, "I bet Eazy wished he had."

Black ain't know what ta say. He just shrugged. Angel gave me one of those "That's a jood one" nods.

That uncomfortable silence was broken when tha only other customer in tha shop, who was sportin a big ol' mushroom cloud 'fro and fell asleep not a minute after he came in, started snorin *louder*. It sounded like somebody was usin a chain saw on some wood.

Black stepped over ta tha brotha and slapped him on tha knee wit' his towel, wakin him up. "Man, this ain't no Holiday Inn!"

Me 'n' Angel laughed as we threw on our jackets.

Angel gave him a brotha hug. "Thanks, Black. Same time next week."

"You got it, brotha."

156

"And stay *Black*, Black!"

Black smiled. "Ha, ain't no other way ta stay." He turned ta me. "Later, Rah."

"Peayce, brotha," I sang, as we brotha-hugged, too.

As me 'n' Angel left, Black returned his attention ta that customer, who had returned ta snorin. "Nigga, you better wake yo' ass up, or you gonna be lookin like Don King!"

APRIL 4th, 10:25 p.m.

I spent tha last two days learnin my lines (I ain't got that many) and waitin fuh my furniture ta arrive. Well, most of it was Li'l Brotha Man's. He got a five-piece full-size bedroom set, a 13-inch TV set, a VCR, a mini-stereo system, a three-shelf bookcase fuh all them books he can't wait ta read, a desk and chair, and a Apple computer wit' a printer (I'm gonna make sure he prepared fuh tha 21st century). I wanted his room, mo' than any other in our place, ta be all hooked up. He's gonna stay wit' me this comin weekend befo' I head back out ta da West Coast (and hopefully, Little Bit will, too). On Sunday he was doin cartwheels from one end of his room ta another and enjoyin hearin his voice echo and bounce off tha walls, so he's gonna be su'prised ta see that almost ev'ry inch of it is filled up. Yeah, I'm gonna spoil him—but just a little bit. (I thought of gettin him a beeper but nixed that; I got myself a cell phone instead so he and ev'rybody else can contact me anytime, especially when I'm on da road.) Not only do he deserve it, I deserve it. Seein that he got luxuries I ain't have, that most folks don't have at his age, gives me mo' pleasure than spendin that green on sumthin fuh myself.

After all that movin, pushin, and liftin, I was exhausted. After talkin ta Little Bit, I was all ready ta turn in early (even tho' I barely slept tha past few nites cuz I was afraid of havin that nightmare again) when I saw it right where I left it—sittin on top of my boom box. I sat at tha edge of my bed, starin at it. Angel had passed it on ta me yesterday. When he told me who he got it from and who made it, I was gonna just throw it away. But... well...I hafta admit, I was curious. And...I don't know... feelin guilty?

I took it out of its white envelope, put it in tha cassette deck, and pressed play.

Hi, Errol. It's David. I know you never liked anyone calling you that, but I always thought it was a classy name, so forgive me just this one time, OK?

I wrote down what I was going to say to you, but you know no one can read my handwriting but me. So I felt the best way would be to tape this message to you. Also, I didn't know if Trey would be able to find you, and if he did, if you would even come to see me.

If you're listening to this…I'm dead. I still can't believe I'm gonna die. The date I'm recording this message is March 2nd. I just had a really nasty bout with pneumonia. The doctor says I was lucky to survive it. But the next time…well, there won't be a next time. My immune system is just about shot, my T-cell count is in the low double-digit range. They say it'll be a miracle if I last another month. So I'm not really sick anymore; I'm dying. There's a difference.

Do I sound like I'm dying? I don't know what a dying person sounds like. I mean, I'm listening to myself talk, and it sounds like me, but I do feel it. And this has got to be the worst way to die. You watch it happen. You smell it happen. You hear it happen. Slowly. I don't recognize myself now; I hate to look in a mirror because I don't know who the person is staring back at me. I'm not the same size or shape, yeah, but it's more than that. This thing just doesn't kill you; it destroys you. I wouldn't wish this on anybody, even though I know there are people who are happy it happened to me (and, no, I wasn't talking about you). I didn't know I had it until it was too late. It all happened so fast. I wanted to tell you but…but I didn't know how to. I kept putting it off until… Well, we were always careful, so you are probably OK. But you should get checked out anyway.

I have a picture of you on my table here in the hospital; it was that night you were wearing that bright yellow shirt and that yellow bandana, sitting on my couch. You looked so jood. We had just come back from seeing Malcolm X. *It turned me on, seeing how excited you got over the movie. We talked about it for hours. I enjoyed that so much. I think that was the first time we were together and didn't have an argument. You stayed the night and slept in my arms. I wish it could've been like that all the time. But I know: I would push. I always had something smart to say. I could be a real bitch. I know that's what you always felt, and it's probably the way you still feel.*

But I just wanted you to know that I am sorry for the way I acted towards you…and him. Yeah, I was trying to start something. I had hoped you two would have a fight about me, that you would leave him and find your way back to me. I waited for you that night…and the next night…and the next… I didn't hear from you, and then I got the undeniable proof that we would never be.

It was the very last time I saw you. It was February last year, the week of Presidents' Day. You were with…him. And your son. At least I think it was your son; he looks just like you. I bet he's gonna break hearts, too. You never introduced me to him; you never even showed me a picture of him. I guess that should have told me how you felt, hunh? Anyway, you all were shopping in the Manhattan Mall. I followed you around for an hour, going from store to store, getting your son shoes and clothes, you and him listening to and buying music, you all getting something to eat at the Food Court. I saw how you all acted…how you looked at him, how he looked at you, how your son looked at the both of you, how you all laughed together. I…I just stood back, away from you all so you wouldn't see me. Then I went home and cried.

I realized right then that I was a fool for holding on to want-

ing you, for wanting you to love me…but not a fool for loving you. I loved you then—and I still do. And, I guess I will…'til the day I die. If you didn't know before, you were really and truly my first and only love.

No matter what happened between us, I am glad you came into my life. Even if you didn't love me back. And I think that is what I was hoping you would do all that time, knowing you wouldn't. That's OK. In some strange way, you made me happy. And I hope that in some way I did the same for you. We had some good…oh, sorry, jood times, didn't we? And I know you won't believe it, but I do hope that you and…you two are happy together for a long time. I saw the love you have for each other; it's so obvious. Am I jealous? Yes. I am jealous of him. I am jealous of what you two have. I am also angry that it isn't me in his place, that I'm not the one giving you what you found in him…that I wasn't the one you could love. But we all need love, we all deserve it—and I hope you keep it.

So, Errol (oops…sorry, that slipped out), stay sexy, sweet, and jood enough to eat (and you know you are, Snuggles…ya know I couldn't resist calling you that just one last time, too). I'll miss you. Maybe you'll miss me, too. I don't know what waits for me on the other side…if there is another side. My mother tells me I'm going to hell since I refused to renounce my lifestyle and accept Christ as my savior. Whatever. You shoulda saw her face when I told her, 'You should know all about hell; you been puttin everyone in your life through it, especially me.' I don't think there is a hell after we die; I think we make our own hell in life. I feel the same way about heaven. I had a little piece of heaven, and you were responsible for it. When I *finally close my eyes for the last time…I have the feeling I won't see or feel anything ever again…that even my spirit won't live on. You die and that's it. If that's so, at least I loved in some way. I wish it was better; I wish it was more than it was. But I'm just glad it was.*

Have a jood life. And jood luck in your career. I hope one day you are on a giant billboard in the middle of Times Square. That would be a sight to see.

"So...you angry wit' me?"

Little Bit was sittin on my sofa. I decided ta tell him at my place, so that if he was angry wit' me, he couldn't tell me ta get tha fuck outa his house. I broke tha news after we ate dinner. We had some Chinese takeout. I— or rather, he—will do some cookin when I get some pots, pans, and dishes ta work wit'.

I could tell he was thinkin real hard: He clasped his hands as if he was about ta pray. "Um, yeah. I *am* angry with you."

"I'm...I'm sorry."

"About what?"

"Lyin about takin tha test."

"That's not what I'm angry about."

"It ain't?"

"No."

"Then why you angry?"

"Because, Pooquie, for the past two weeks you've been carrying this around, keeping it to yourself, and you didn't have to."

"But I...I ain't wanna worry you."

"So you just worry yourself about it? Hmm...this explains why you've been so...restless. Distant. Disinterested. And why I haven't seen you the past four days."

Yeah, I had ta keep that distance. I spent much of that time ridin my bike (sumthin I hadn't done since I left Mel's 10 months ago) and agonizin over what I was gonna say ta him, even rehearsin my lines in my bathroom mirror. I decided a coupla times that not only was I not gonna tell him, I wasn't even gonna find out what tha results was. I was afraid of losin him; I couldn't imagine what my world would be like wit'out him. But I also knew that, no matter how hard it was and no matter what might happen, I had ta be straight up wit' him—and myself. Besides, I wouldn'ta been able ta hide from some shit like this. Ev'rybody—meanin Little Bit, Moms, Sunshine, L'il Brotha Man, even Angel and my Pops—knows when sumthin is eatin me up. And sumthin like this could eat me alive.

He frowned. "This *also* explains why I found that video behind the sofa."

I'm guilty. He wanted ta have a Denzel movie day last Saturday. *Ricochet* and *Mississippi Masala*, I could handle. But *Philadelphia*? Now, you know there was no way I was gonna be watchin that. Tha last thing I needed ta see was Tom Hanks dyin of AIDS. So when Little Bit was makin popcorn, I hid tha video. I meant ta "find it" when he took 'em back later that nite but fuhgot about it. I guess he went searchin fuh it, especially since tha video store had proof he took out three movies, not two, and would charge him fuh it.

I bent down in fronta him. I placed my left hand on top of his right hand. "Little Bit, I just ain't know how ta tell ya…what ta tell ya…"

"And if you were positive, would you have known what to tell me? Would you have known *how* to tell me?"

"*Hell*, yeah. Shit, I ain't wanna kick it wit' you *not* knowin. Ain't no way I could, knowin I got it."

"Why did you tell me?"

"Why?"

"Yes, why. After all, you didn't have to tell me anything at this point. You're negative. So there was no need to tell me you took the test or that you lied about taking it before."

"I…I guess I felt you had a right ta know, anyway."

"Why?"

"Cuz, you my Baby and I love you. Don't you know that by now?"

He folded his hand inta mine. "Yes. Yes, I do."

"I mean, all I could think was, *What if I got a plus sign? What if I gave it ta you? And what if I lost you cuz of it?* I guess I coulda said nuthin, but…this is sumthin I had ta release. I ain't wanna keep that a secret from you no mo'."

"Hmm…what made you get tested?"

"Eazy."

"E?"

"Yeah. If it can happen ta him, and he not know it…you just never know."

He nodded. "True."

Silence.

"Is that what your nightmare was about?" he asked.

"Yeah."

"You wanna talk about it?"

He sat back. I lounged across tha sofa, and my head found its place on his lap. I told him about my dream: how I was outside a church and figured it musta been Eazy's funeral cuz there was TV crews and folks wit' signs sayin R.I.P., EAZY and WE'LL MISS U, EAZY standin behind police barricades. I went inside, and it was standin room only. Some minister was offerin words of comfort while a organist played. I got on tha line ta view tha body and as I got ta tha front rows, there was my Moms wit' her head on my Pop's shoulder, Angel wit' his face buried in his hands, and Sunshine 'n' Li'l Brotha Man bein held by him. They was all cryin. Then I looked in tha casket and saw why.

It was *me*.

Little Bit stroked my head. "Oh, Pooquie. That's awful."

"Tell me about it. I just knew I couldn't tell you about it cuz you woulda been askin some questions."

"You know I would've."

"You sure you ain't angry wit' me about lyin?"

He kissed my head. "Yes, I'm sure. I mean, how can I be when...when I lied to you, too?"

Little Bit...*lie*? I mean, he ain't perfect, I know, but I never woulda thought, of all tha things he would do wrong, he'd do that.

I shifted ta face him. "You lied?"

He was embarrassed. "Yes, I did. I...I've never taken the test."

"You never took it?"

"No."

"Why you lie about?"

"Well...I said I took it because...because you're supposed to be up on things like that. I guess I didn't want to seem ignorant. It...it scares me to death."

I sat up and wrapped him up in my arms. "I know how you feel."

"I...I always wanted to do it with the person I am with. But it wasn't the kind of thing most of the men I've dated would entertain. I asked a couple of them whether they had taken one, and they were insulted that I even asked them. As you know, it isn't exactly a topic folks like to discuss."

"Yeah, I know."

"And there were a few who knew they were so clean

that they didn't have to use a condom."

"And you let 'em?"

"*Hell,* no. I've did a lot of stupid things for lust and love in my lifetime, but laying down my life wasn't one of them. If he thought he was too jood for a condom, he wasn't jood enough for me."

"Uh…do you wanna take one?" I asked.

Silence.

"You think I should?" he almost whispered.

"Yeah. At least you ain't gonna go thru it alone. It's better ta know."

Silence again.

"Um…what if…what if it comes back positive?" His voice was shakin.

I ain't miss a beat. "Then we deal wit' it."

He pulled back from me. He searched my eyes. "We?"

"Yeah. We."

He wrapped his arms around my neck; I gripped him tighter around his waist. We kissed. I mean, *really* kissed. We hadn't kissed like that in a couple of weeks, but it felt like a couple of years.

He settled against my chest. "Thanks, Pooquie."

"Fuh what?"

"For being you."

"Thank *you,* Baby, fuh bein tha kinda man I can come ta wit' this."

"It takes one to know one. And thanks for being there."

"Anytime, Little Bit. Anytime."

Hearts beatin in silence.

"Um...since we tellin secrets..." I knew I didn't hafta go there, but I wanted ta have ev'rythang out on tha table. I ain't want there ta be no su'prises fuh him, fuh me, fuh us in tha future.

So I told him about messin around wit' Malice (and I made sure he knew it was *just* messin around), but ain't tell him his name.

Then I pleaded my case. "Now, I wouldn't blame you if you angry wit' me. And I guess I couldn't blame you if you decided you ain't wanna see me for a while...or ever again. But I'm sorry, Baby. I really am sorry. Ya know I would never just go out and do sumthin ta hurt you. I know it's gonna sound *stoopid*, but...it just happened. But it ain't never gonna happen again." Hearin me say it out loud ta him...I think that convinced me that it wouldn't. Wit' Malice or anybody else.

He was quiet. *Too* quiet. He didn't even move. I wasn't expectin him ta scream, throw shit (not that there was anything ta throw) and carry on. But I expected *sumthin*.

Then...

He sighed. "Well...I guess we're both entitled to an indiscretion."

Hunh?

"It happened when you were in L.A. We...we went dancing. To a concert. He cooked us dinner. And...I stayed the night with him."

KER-PLUNK.

"But it was only a moment in time. He only caught my attention for a brief moment. You've caught and still have my heart." He lifted his head. He looked at me. "Can you forgive me?"

Now, I was *truly* in shock. Goes ta show you don't really know what yo' baybay is capable of. I mean, I always knew that if anybody was gonna do sumthin fucked up (like fuck around) that could fuck up what we got, it was gonna be me. It never even occurred ta me that while I was workin that *naaasty* groove wit' Malice or bein pawed and passed around by them Mack-truck mutha-fuckas that Little Bit coulda been doin tha same thang or sumthin like it back home. I *really* wanted ta ask if they fucked each other—I mean, what does "stay the night" mean?—but that was sumthin I really *didn't* wanna know. Besides, he woulda said so if they did. And even if it *did* happen, it woulda just been fuckin, not jood lovin like I can give him.

And while it did sting me a lot ta hear it, and it wrecked me ta know he was wit' somebody else in *any* way, I knew I could say, "Yeah, I can. Can you fuhgive *me*?"

"Of course I can. We'll make mistakes—missteps." He glared at me. "Let's just not make them a habit."

"Ha, you ain't gotta worry about that."

"Uh...you sure there isn't any other secret you'd like to get off your chest?" he quizzed.

I ain't know what he was talkin about, and that look on my face said it all.

"You know...about *us*."

Ah...*now* I knew what he was talkin about. "Now, why you wanna even go there?" I grinned.

"Because I wouldn't be me if I didn't."

"Well, it's funny you *did* go there. I think my Pops know."

He was…I guess tha word is…*startled*. And it wasn't about my Pops knowin. I know he never expected me ta call him that, ta identify him that way. He was also happy ta hear it. He smiled. "What makes you think…your Pops knows?" he asked with pride.

"He wants all of us ta come over ta his house in June ta celebrate me 'n' Li'l Brotha Man's birthdays. And he included *you* in that all."

"Did he?"

"Yeah. He called you my *friend*."

"*Really?*"

"Yeah. He told me not ta fuck up all tha jood thangz I got goin on, like he did."

"Hmm…I guess he *has* been watching you real close. Or…it could just be that…he knows his own son."

I shrugged.

"Well, if *he* knows, and he hasn't really been in your life…"

I stopped him befo' he went any further cuz we been down this road many, *many* times. "Yeah, I know, I know. I can't say it's gonna happen tomorrow, but…it's gonna happen."

I had never said *that* befo', either. It's always been "I don't know what ta tell them" or "I don't know when it would be a jood time" or "It's too soon" or (that old-standby) "They would *never* understand." But I think now *I* understand. I don't know. Sumthin's changed. I felt…diff'rent.

I think Little Bit could feel it, too. He looked in my eyes. He smiled. He gave me one of dem double-*L* (light 'n' luscious) kisses.

Hearts beatin in silence, again.

He sighed; it was a content one. "You know…I think everything that's happened…it was some kind of test for the both of us."

"Whatcha mean?"

"Being tempted…questioning our own commitment to each other…to ourselves…facing our own imperfections…*and* immortality…I guess…I guess this might be God's way of saying 'If you can conquer this together, you can conquer anything.'"

I still ain't believe in no God, but given all I had been thru in tha past coupla weeks, I was willin ta go along wit' that assessment. "I'd hafta agree."

"I guess one could call it growing pains."

I squeezed him. "Well, I can handle growin pains. So long as I know I still got you."

We kissed like *that*, again.

He kneeled on tha sofa. "Well, my Chocolate Drop Daddy, I think it's time to catch up on *thangz*, make up for lost time, don't cha think?" he growled, battin them eyes as he almost ripped tha buttons off my shirt.

I grabbed two heapin handfuls of his azz and squeezed it. "Oh, *yeah*, Baby. It's on."

"Daddy?"

"Yeah, my man?"

"I been thinking."

I smiled. "Oh, have you?"

"Uh-huh."

"About what?"

"About what I wanna be when I grow up."

"Oh, yeah?"

"Uh-huh. My teacher, Mr. Gianelli, told us to think about it over the weekend. It's my homework. And I know what I wanna be."

"You know already?"

"Yes."

175

"But you only been outa school 10 minutes. And it's only *Thursday*. You don't wanna think about it 'til Sunday?"

"No."

"A'ight, then. Whatcha wanna be?"

"An as-tro-naut!"

"An astronaut?"

"Yes!" he squealed.

"You know what that is?"

"Uh-huh. That's a man—or a lady—who travels on a spaceship."

"Right. But why you wanna be that?"

"Be-cause, Daddy, an astronaut gets to go into the u-nee-verse!"

"'The u-nee-verse'?"

"Uh-huh."

"And what is that?"

"Come on, Daddy, you have to know what the u-nee-verse is. It's the stars, the planets, the moon, the sun…*the galaxy*!"

"Ah, a'ight. So why you wanna go out there?"

"Because it looks fun."

"It does?"

"Uh-huh. You get all dressed up in a space suit and a helmet, and you just float off and away. I wanna walk in space like the man Mr. Gianelli told us about."

"What man?"

"The first Black man to walk in space. You know his name, Daddy?"

I did, but I faked it. "Nah, I don't. Do you?"

He grinned. "Yes, I do. His name is Bern-ahrd Harris. He's a doctor. He made history, Daddy."

"Yeah, he did."

"I wanna make history, too."

"And how you plan on doin that?"

"I'm gonna be the *second* Black man to walk in space!" he declared.

I chuckled. "You are, hunh?"

"Yes. I wanna go down in history books, just like Bern-ahrd Harris. And I want you to be proud of me, Daddy."

"I'm already proud of you, Li'l Brotha Man."

"You are?"

"Of course I am."

"Why? I didn't do anything great like walk in space."

"You *do* do great things."

"I do?"

"Yeah."

"Like what?"

"Like bein yo'self. That's enuff ta make me proud."

"What do you mean?"

"I mean that you ain't gotta be no astronaut fuh me ta be proud of you."

"I don't?"

"No, you don't."

"But it's something special, Daddy."

"Yeah, I guess it is. But you already sumthin special cuz you you, my man."

"Because I'm...me?" He pointed ta himself.

"Yeah. You ain't special cuz of what you do in life. It's

who you are that counts. And you a smart little boy."

"I am?"

"Yeah. And you smart enuff ta be an astronaut. But you should become one cuz you wanna, not cuz you think it's gonna make me proud of you. No matter what you do when you grow up, I'm gonna be proud of you."

Yeah, tha tip of that left thumb went inta his mouth. "Oh...so, if I don't become an astronaut, you still be proud of me?"

"Of course I will. If it's what you wanna do, do it."

"Um...I still wanna do it."

"A'ight."

"And you know what I'm gonna do when I go into space, Daddy?"

"What?"

"I'm gonna find out if E.T. made it home!"

I laughed. "If anybody can do that, Li'l Brotha Man, I know you can."

I tweaked his nose. We smiled at each other.